Riley hadn't been looking for a wife. . .

. . .but something about Nettie brought out feelings in him he'd never have guessed he had.

All the fight seemed to be gone from her, and he almost missed it. "I'd like for us to work toward a better relationship."

"In what way?"

Riley felt the back of his neck grow wet. Never had a woman affected him like this. "Friends first, then I thought we could look into the possibility of God wanting us to have a real married life."

For the first time, he saw Nettie appear not to know what to say.

"I mean He put us together for a reason," Riley continued, "and I hope it's not to kill each other fighting." He meant for his latter remark to be funny, but she didn't even smile. When he looked into her face with the lantern light dancing off her hair, he caught his breath. A man could do a whole lot worse than Nettie Franklin O'Connor. Right then, Riley couldn't think of a more beautiful woman in all of Nebraska.

"Quarreling makes me furious at myself," she said. "I don't have a terrible temper. It's simply the words come flying out of my mouth before I can stop them."

"I used to have a bad way about settling disputes, but that's not God honoring. What do you say? Can we give this marriage a try?"

DIANN MILLS lives in Houston, Texas, with her husband, Dean. They have four adult sons. She wrote from the time she could hold a pencil, but not seriously until God made it clear that she should write for Him. After three years of serious writing, her first book Rehoboth won favorite Heartsong Presents historical for 1998. Other publishing credits include magazine articles and short stories, devotionals, poetry, and internal writing for her church. She is an active church choir member, leads a ladies Bible study, and is a church librarian.

Books by DiAnn Mills

HEARTSONG PRESENTS

HP291—Rehoboth
HP322—Country Charm
HP374—The Last Cotillion
HP394—Equestrian Charm
HP410—The Color of Love
HP441—Cassidy's Charm
HP450—Love in Pursuit
HP504—Mail-Order Husband
HP513—Licorice Kisses
HP527—The Turncoat

Don't miss out on any of our super romances. Write to us at the following address for information on our newest releases and club information.

Heartsong Presents Readers' Service
PO Box 721
Uhrichsville, OH 44683

Temporary Husband

DiAnn Mills

Heartsong Presents

To Russell and Penney Andrew.
Thank you for your love and support!

A note from the Author:
I love to hear from my readers! You may correspond with me
by writing:

> **DiAnn Mills**
> **Author Relations**
> **PO Box 719**
> **Uhrichsville, OH 44683**

ISBN 1-58660-926-2

TEMPORARY HUSBAND

Our mission is to publish and distribute inspirational products offering
exceptional value and biblical encouragement to the masses.

All Scripture quotations are taken from the King James Version of the
Bible.

one

Nebraska
July 1885

Nettie Franklin paused to hear the lively laughter and shivered. She picked up her skirts, arched her back, and stepped through the creaking, swinging doors of Mesquite's only saloon. She gasped at the show of decadence before her. In the dim lighting, men peered into cards as though they held the meaning of life. Base women with exposed bosoms and glaring face paint sat on their laps. She drew in a sharp breath and held it when the father of one of her students slapped his cards on the table and lifted a glass of something to his lips. She suspected he wasn't drinking water.

Her gaze swept around the room and rested on a tall, narrow, table like structure adjacent to the swinging doors. A middle-aged man with dark, thinning hair stood behind it and laughed with the men on the opposite side. Liquor! She smelled it sharply along with a musty odor that attacked her sensitive stomach. Liquor gleamed wickedly from bottles and glasses. To Nettie, it was the root of one of the worst sins known to man. Did these poor people not know the depths to which they had fallen?

Trembling, yet knowing she could not back down, Nettie craned her neck and cleared her throat, but no one noticed her at all. "Ah hem." This time she managed to gain a bit of attention.

"Yes, Ma'am," the man behind the long table said. He plopped a bottle onto the top and poured some into a glass for another man. She heard the golden-colored liquid gurgle.

"What can I do for you? Need a drink? Looking for your husband?" He turned to a man across from him. "Here's your whiskey, Frank."

Appalled at the sight before her, Nettie rushed forward, nearly tripping, and grabbed the drink before the man could bring the glass to his lips.

"Sir, your soul is at stake if you partake of this devil's potion," she said. Satisfied the Lord sat on His throne praising her good works, Nettie willed her heart to cease its thunderous pounding.

"Frank, she has you there," the man who served the liquor said.

Frank said nothing, but the fellow standing beside him clapped a hand across his back. She felt a spark of hope. How she despised confrontation, but she must obey her God-given calling.

"Ma'am," Frank began and pushed his hat back from his forehead. "I'm gonna overlook what you just did given you're a woman and this summer heat has about done me in. Now, I suggest you hand over my drink and go on back home to your family."

"She's a spinster," a woman said. Her raucous laugh infected the saloon.

Frank chuckled. "Then I gather she don't know no better, so I'll go easy on her."

Nettie smoothed her dark skirt. "I'd like to talk to you about the wickedness of drinking."

Frank, a thin fellow, lifted a brow. "I think you'd better loosen your fingers on my drink before I forget you're a woman, although you're a pretty one to be so ornery."

Her heart roared in her ears. "What do you intend to—"

He reached for the glass held tightly between her fingers, but she took a step back. "Sir, you don't understand."

"Ma'am, if you want a drink, I'll buy you one, but give me mine."

Nettie's knees shook, and suddenly she noticed everyone stared at her. She felt their scrutiny piercing her bones. "S—s—sir," she stuttered, "the Bible has much to say about the evils of drunkenness."

"Ma'am, give the customer his whiskey," said the man behind the tall table.

Frank faced her squarely. His granite like features held fearful implications. "This is your last warning."

"Easy," the man who supplied the drinks said. "The judge is in the back; I'll fetch him to handle this."

Frank glared at Nettie. "For the last time, hand me my drink."

Her tongue thickened, and the words refused to come. Rather than admit defeat, she emptied the glass's contents on the floor. The room resembled a tomb.

"Nettie Franklin! What do you think you're doing?" The familiar voice of Albert Balsh, the saloon's owner and judge for Mesquite and the surrounding county, echoed in her ears. "Give that man his drink."

She felt a bit more confident. The Bible said to love everyone, and she must show her love by protecting these sinful people from the indiscretion of their ways. Besides, the judge wouldn't allow any of them to hurt her. She handed Frank the empty glass and offered a shaky smile. The irate man stood there, his eyebrows twitching.

"Judge, she poured my drink on the floor."

Nettie whirled around to face Judge Balsh. She met his towering frame and stiffened, believing in her heart he too must be convicted of his ways. "I surely did. The evils of drunkenness—"

"The last thing I want to hear is you spouting off Scripture to customers." The judge clenched his fists. His face reddened like midsummer tomatoes.

"But you will hear me." She glanced about. "All of you are bound to everlasting condemnation—"

The judge waved his hand in front of her face. "That's enough, Nettie. Pay for the man's drink and get out of here. My customers don't need you harassing them."

Nettie stamped her foot on the wooden floor. "I will not. It's my responsibility to inform these people of the evils of this place. Look around you, Judge. How can God bless them when they are. . .are. . .involved with drinking and ungodly behavior?"

The judge pointed his finger at her. "I'm no saint, Miss Franklin, but it seems to me this isn't the way to persuade people to your way of thinking." He looked out at the small crowd. "Somebody go get the sheriff."

"The sheriff." Nettie's voice cracked. *Is this what the Bible meant by facing persecution?*

"Yes, Ma'am. I'm having you arrested for disturbing my peaceful business."

❧

Nettie stared at the wooden walls of her cell. They seemed to move in closer as she felt the weight of her plight tightening around her throat. *Calm yourself. The judge will have you released soon.*

She sat on a rope cot, the only piece of furniture in the dingy chamber. The blanket at the end clung to horse manure and other unnamed filth. A spider scampered across the cot's equator. The citizens of Mesquite had prided themselves in this jail. They'd built it entirely of wood except for the metal bars the blacksmith had fashioned to keep the prisoners inside.

She attempted to look at the good side of things, if there existed a good side to sitting in jail for trying to save souls.

The cell reeked, not like a soddie with the odor of earth, bugs, and worms, but of unwashed bodies and the sin of what caused them to be incarcerated in the first place. Of course, snakes couldn't crawl through the roof and drop onto the floor or wasps make their nest in the most obscure places as they did in a soddie, but this cell reverberated with signs of unconfessed sin. In short it smelled of men, because proper ladies were not to grace the inside of such an establishment. Unless you had strong opinions about the temperance movement and you angered the judge who owned the town's saloon.

What would her mother say? She'd be disgraced. For once, Nettie realized the blessings of having her mother living with the Lord.

Swallowing her tears, Nettie willed her mind and body not to worry about what others said. Worse yet, what would happen to her? Memories of the judge's twitching eyes flitted across her mind.

"Take Miss Nettie to jail and I'll tend to her later," he'd said to the sheriff. "Lock her up and pocket the key. I don't want to set eyes on her again."

"Can't keep her there forever, Judge," Sheriff Kroft said. Tobacco stained what few teeth he had, and if not for the badge, he'd easily be mistaken for an outlaw.

"Sure I can. I'm the judge, aren't I?"

Now, as those words repeated in Nettie's weary head, panic took root like a nasty weed.

Most times, Nettie kept her sympathies to herself, unless the Lord had advice about the subject—like the temperance movement. Unfortunately she often said things without thinking. Later she'd apologize, and then it would take months before she could speak to the person without feeling humiliated. Sometimes those she offended held a perpetual grudge.

Today might have been one of those times. Judge Balsh didn't take too kindly to her interference in his business. Money meant a lot to him, but what he took particular offense to was her friendship with his wife, Maudie Mae.

"I'd do most anything to keep you from Maudie Mae," the judge had said earlier.

Shaking her head, Nettie refuted her thoughts. She had

merely been following the Scripture's precepts so well pointed out by those leading the temperance movement. She desperately wanted courage like "Mother" Eliza Daniel Stewart possessed to stand up to those who did not understand the sinful nature of liquor. How grand to think that she, Nettie Franklin, might be written about in the history books as a daring woman who persisted against the harms of strong drink.

Alcohol must be prohibited in the United States or God might pass judgment on the country. Nettie had found the courage to approach the judge's customers and employees in hopes they'd forsake strong drink. She believed one day the town of Mesquite would thank her for taking a stand to preserve the righteousness of their community. The entire state of Nebraska would hear of her prowess.

Before coming to Mesquite, Nettie had been a midwife in nearby Archerville. She'd birthed a lot of beautiful babies in the community, but she really wanted to teach. Archerville already had an excellent teacher, and the community had no need for two people in that profession. When Nettie learned Mesquite needed someone to school their children, she prayerfully applied and then secured the position. Leaving good friends had been difficult, but she wanted more for her life than growing old birthing babies for other folks. She'd had a difficult time accepting the heartache of never finding a husband or having a family of her own.

In Mesquite she met Maudie Mae, an upstanding member of the school board, whose grown sons lived in Lincoln. Nettie and Maudie Mae had so much in common: loving children, knitting, Christian values—and a strong dislike for alcohol. They discussed that aspect of their relationship at great length and even formed a small Bible study related to the prohibition of drinking. To Nettie's amazement and shock, she learned Judge Balsh owned the town's saloon. She saw it as a serious obstacle, and Maudie Mae had looked for a way to dissolve her husband's business for a long time.

"Why, it's embarrassing," Maudie Mae said on repeated occasions.

Although the judge was not given to strong drink, the saloon had kept him from home too long. Besides, he encouraged the habit in others. Maudie Mae believed Nettie's willingness to take action came as answered prayer.

Nettie heard the door of the jail open and close. She recognized Maudie Mae's high-pitched voice and looked up to see her dear friend.

"Don't you dare tell me I can't see Nettie," Maudie Mae said. "Besides, she's right there."

Sheriff Oliver Kroft scratched his bald head while chewing a jaw full of tobacco.

"The judge said Miss Franklin wasn't supposed to have any visitors," the sheriff said.

"I know what that means, Oliver." Maudie Mae's tone escalated. Some found her voice irritating. Nettie overlooked the grating sound, although it reminded her of fingernails scraping across a chalkboard. Nettie needed a friend, and Maudie Mae understood her views on temperance.

"Then kindly let me get back to my job," Oliver replied.

"Humph. Looks to me like your work consists of reading dime novels."

Silence. Nettie held her breath, waiting to hear Oliver's reply.

"Cat got your tongue, Oliver? Now, unlock my friend's cell so I can talk to her."

A moment later, Maudie Mae stood in front of Nettie without the metal bars between them. Nettie clung to the tall, bony woman while tears streamed down her face.

"It'll be all right." Maudie Mae patted Nettie's back. "Tell me what you did to make the judge so mad."

"I–I only wanted those people to see how wrong it was to

drink whiskey." Nettie sobbed and explained the happenings at the saloon the best she could. "So you see, I did God's bidding, and now I'm being persecuted."

"Honey, Honey, Honey," Maudie Mae said in a singsong tone that usually drove Nettie to distraction. "Organizing women to pray for loved ones who are prone to drink and singing hymns outside the saloon are good ways to continue the temperance movement." She hesitated and drew herself up to her full five-feet-ten height. "But sashaying into the judge's saloon and grabbing a drink from one of his customers is sure to bring my husband's wrath down hard on you."

Nettie swallowed hard. "You mean, he is serious-mad?"

Maudie Mae's bulging eyes opened wide, and she nodded. "I haven't been graced with his presence, but I know how he feels about our activities."

"You mean. . .you mean I might not get out of here for a few more hours?"

"How about a few years?"

Nettie gasped. "Why, he can't do that."

"Honey, Honey, Honey, he's the judge."

Nettie grasped her friend's hand. "Please, oh please, Maudie Mae, won't you talk to him?"

She moistened her lips. "The only thing sure to settle the judge is if you give up the temperance movement altogether."

"I can't! It's my divine calling." Nettie covered her heart with her hand. How could Maudie Mae suggest such a thing?

"Then we'll have to think of something else."

"But what? Maudie Mae, I must not have been praying hard enough. I should have shouted God's Word at the top of my lungs." She shook her head. "God loves all of His children, and He elected me to be His instrument."

Maudie Mae touched her finger to her nose as she always did when pondering something. "You know I love you, Nettie. You're my best friend, and I believe wholeheartedly in the temperance principles. I know drinking is an abomination of the devil. Why, it causes fine men to spend all their hard-earned money, fight like heathens, and it leads to suffering families. The Bible says a whole lot about drunkenness, and I have all them Scripture verses memorized just like you, but making people mad won't solve a thing."

"What do you mean? Someone needs to tell them of their sinful ways."

"Rightfully so, but friendly, sweet persuasion goes further than condemnation. Anyway, my way of reasoning tells me making enemies doesn't help a thing."

"Surely you aren't suggesting I apologize?"

"Hear me out, Nettie. You can tell the man you're sorry for taking his drink, then swallow your pride and make amends with the judge."

Nettie felt a twinge of truth ring in her ears. Maybe there was a better way.

"Remember the woman at the well?" Maudie Mae asked.

"Yes, I–I do." The Lord wasn't condemning at all, but loving.

"Well, just dwell on that be—"

"Mrs. Balsh, I see the judge headin' this way. You best get yourself out the back door," the sheriff said. His boots hit the floor hard.

Before Maudie Mae spoke another word, she stepped from the cell and shut the door.

"Are you going to help me?" Near hysteria rose in Nettie's voice. "I don't think I can stand it much longer in here. And what will I do come nightfall?"

"Hush," her friend said.

"Promise me you'll talk to the judge."

"I'll try." Maudie Mae tossed over her shoulder. "Can't promise anything, but I'll try."

two

Riley O'Connor hunched over the saddle of his chestnut mare, which had carried him from his ranch in Montana to Nebraska. Every muscle in his body ached. He craved about three days of sleep, but that comfort might never happen, at least not until he rode home.

Mesquite, a town he hadn't visited for more than four years, lay just ahead on the desolate, dusty road. Hopefully everyone there had forgotten the circumstances the last time he lived among those fine people. Back then he resembled more of a twister than an upstanding Christian citizen. Riley cringed. He'd torn the sleepy town apart with his drinking and fighting. Maybe Judge Balsh didn't sit on the bench any longer. They hadn't parted on friendly terms. In fact, if Riley's memory served him correctly, he and the judge clearly despised each other at the time. Riley had changed, but unless the judge held court with the Lord, he didn't know about Riley's new heart.

Shifting in the saddle, Riley realized if he hadn't been in need of supplies and owed a man a word of thanks, he'd have ridden right past Mesquite. The idea of good folks recollecting his past wild ways didn't settle well. He couldn't blame them. Back then his name put a bad taste in the mouths of every decent man around, and the only women who'd give him a second look weren't the settling-down type. But those were the same reasons why he needed to visit a man who lived in these parts.

Riley had left Archerville shortly after being jilted by a widow. She'd rejected his marriage proposal and married the homeliest man he'd ever seen. The man hadn't known a thing about farming, but he caught on fast. The last Riley heard, the couple had four children. At the time, devastation and anger nearly destroyed Riley. He hadn't been accustomed to being turned down by any woman.

So he rode on to Mesquite, looking to start over. He'd been so full of hate and revenge back then—mostly toward himself—and he'd desperately wanted someone to put him out of his misery. He worked hard all day for his money, then night after night he drank it up until his temper kicked in and he picked a fight. Too many days he woke up in jail with a hammering headache and unaccountable bruises.

He ran a finger along a deep scar on the right side of his face. The ugly red mark trailed from below his eye to his jaw. Drinking and fighting had caused the disfigurement, but the incident had also changed his heart and his life forever. Whenever he felt tempted to return to his old ways, he recalled the events that led him to the Lord.

On the night he received the gash to his face, he'd been drinking heavily. As was his usual manner, he looked around for a fight. Didn't matter who, just a body he could hammer his fists into. His mind whirled, and the floor spun.

"Why don't you call it a night?" the bartender asked.

"Who are you to tell me when I should quit?" Riley snarled and wiped his mouth with the back of his hand.

The man anchored his palms on the bar. "I'm not telling you anything. I'm suggesting you go home and sleep this off."

"I'll leave when I'm ready and not one minute sooner."

The bartender clenched his jaw. "I'm not serving you any more whiskey."

Riley pounded his fist onto the bar and finished his shot of liquor. "Ain't my money any good? I can pay."

"I know you can, but I'm tired of you picking fights and busting up the place."

Riley grabbed the man by his shirt collar. "Pour me another drink before I lay into you."

"Leave him alone, Riley," a soft voice said behind him.

Riley whipped his attention to one of the women who worked there. She'd been nice to him a few times. "Stay out of this, Faye. The sight of you makes me sick."

Three men stood, men he'd fought and licked on previous nights. One of them said, "You don't talk to a lady like that."

"I know." Riley laughed. "She ain't no lady." He didn't even know the men's names.

"Step outside," the man said. "We'll settle this in the street."

Riley stumbled through the swinging doors. He managed a wild punch into the air. Something hit him alongside the head, and he fell. Riley remembered nothing else until he awoke in jail. His head pounded worse than he could ever recall, and his face felt like someone had set him on fire. He moved, and the pain in his arm nearly caused him to black out.

I can't go on like this. I just want to die and forget about this awful life.

"Riley O'Connor," a raspy voice said.

He tried to open his eyes, but pain shot down his face the moment he moved a muscle to respond. From the smells, he must have vomited all over himself.

"Don't try to talk or open your eyes, just listen to me." Riley obeyed. He hurt too badly not to.

"Last night you nearly bled to death when somebody sliced your face. I found you in the street and brought you here. Figured nobody could do you any more damage with you behind bars. I stitched up your face the best I could, but you'll have a nasty scar. Then there's the matter of your broken arm. I set it, but it will take awhile for it to mend."

If strength had soared through Riley's arms, he'd have grabbed the man by the throat and asked him why he didn't let him die in the street. Riley had nothing going for him, no purpose but to live from one drunk to another.

"Why," Riley said, biting back the agony in his battle-ridden body. "I just want to die."

The man coughed. "I've lived a lot longer than you have, young man, and seen many things. I've learned that no one has the right to take his own life. God's got a plan for you. I suggest you start listenin' to Him instead of that devil water you've been drinking."

"Why?" *Just what I need, a preacher.*

"Is that the only word you know? Well, I'll tell you, Riley. The Creator of the universe didn't put you here to drink yourself crazy and fight every night. He has something special in mind. You'd best be putting some serious thought as to where you'll be spending your eternity."

I know where—and it's mighty hot.

"So I'm leaving this Bible for you to read. Looks like you won't be able to work for awhile anyway."

Just leave me and take your Bible with you. I ain't interested.

Riley heard the metal door of the cell close and the old man shuffle across the jail floor. Hours later he opened his eyes and stared at the ceiling. How many mornings had he awakened in this dingy hole? He recalled the old man's words. Had he dreamed about him? The Bible lay on the floor beside him, proof that the visit had taken place. Riley didn't even know the old man's name.

After a few hours, Judge Balsh came by. "Riley O'Connor, I wished them men would have done you in for good last night. So I'm telling you straight. You can mend a few days in this cell, then ride out of here and don't come back. If I ever see you again in this town, I'll make sure you end up in the state prison."

Riley didn't reply. He knew the judge didn't make idle threats. A few days later, he mounted his chestnut mare and rode out of town with nothing but the old man's Bible. Maybe he could sell it for a drink.

Alone on the trail, Riley took to reading the Bible at night around a fire. He'd never heard a thing about God before, and curiosity kept him turning pages and rereading those passages he didn't understand. One night he stumbled onto the book of Romans. He thumbed through the pages until his attention rested on chapter three, verse twenty-three: "For all have sinned, and come short of the glory of God."

Riley shook his head. Then why bother reading about God and what He wanted for people, if no one stood a chance? He read a little farther, still confused. Then he reached chapter eight. From the first verse, he began to read: "There is therefore now no condemnation to them which are in Christ Jesus, who walk not after the flesh, but after the Spirit."

Riley didn't understand any of it. He needed help. He asked the Lord to explain the things he'd read, and as he did, he realized this marked the first time in his life he'd ever talked to God.

Suddenly the words seemed to come alive. "If God be for us, who can be against us?" Riley read until the embers died in the fire, and when the last spark left him alone in the dark, he gave his life to Jesus Christ. And he hadn't strayed since.

From there he rode to Montana, where he found a job working as a hired hand on a ranch. He worked just like the Bible said—as though he worked for the Lord—and read the Bible at night. Saving money came easy when he didn't drink it up. When a sizeable piece of land came up for sale, the owner sold it to Riley based on his trustworthiness. Riley prospered and gave back to God a tithe just like the Bible instructed.

Riley ushered his mind to the present and pushed back his hat to view the sights of Mesquite. The sun had begun its descent, and in a few hours he'd be sleeping under the stars somewhere outside of the quiet town. The sights were much the same, with the bank, a general store, a barber and undertaker, a new boardinghouse, a livery stable, the jail, and the saloon. He shook the guilt wanting to take over his senses. Riley knew those feelings didn't come from God. One of his reasons for coming here was to find the old man with the raspy voice. Odd, Riley hadn't seen him when he lived in Mesquite before, but most of Riley's associates were the rougher ones.

The sound of his horse clopping down the dusty street shared with pigs and stray dogs left him a bit uneasy. *Are You sure You want me here, Lord?*

"Why if it isn't Riley O'Connor," a man said and waved.

Riley swung his gaze toward the man and recognized him instantly. "Good afternoon, Sheriff Kroft." He pulled his mare to a halt alongside the sheriff and stuck out his hand. "Fine day here, don't you think?"

Oliver Kroft's mouth fell agape. "It. . .surely is."

"I won't be here but a few hours," Riley said. "I need a few provisions, a hot meal, and I'm looking for a man." He smiled, hoping the sheriff saw the change in him. "You might be able to help me there. I need to thank him proper for a good deed."

Sheriff Kroft raised a brow. "Uh, what's the name?"

"I don't know. He's old with a raspy voice. In fact, he doctored me before Judge Balsh asked me to leave town, and he gave me a Bible."

The sheriff tilted his head and eyed him rather strangely. "I remember that old man who tended you that day. He doesn't come around much, and I'm not sure exactly where he lives—if he's even still alive." He spat tobacco juice onto the dry street. "I recollect his name is Abe Wilkins."

Although disappointed not to get more information, Riley realized at least he had a name. "Thanks, Sheriff. Maybe someone at the general store will know where I can find him." He swung down from his mare and tied the horse to a hitching post. When he felt the sheriff's eyes staring at him, he added, "Like I said, I'll only be a few hours. If I can't find Abe Wilkins, I'll still bed down outside of town."

The sheriff nodded. "Judge Balsh is still here."

Riley understood the sheriff's unspoken warning—make the stay as short as possible.

Inside the general store, he saw the canned food items were still arranged by size on the shelves. Yard goods for the ladies lined up on the right side, with farm and feed supplies stacked in the back. Since his departure, the owner had added another room with more goods and a post office.

After he learned the proprietor didn't know where Abe Wilkins lived, Riley purchased enough provisions for the days ahead and packed them in his saddlebags. He sauntered down the street to the livery stable, where he made arrangements to feed and groom his horse.

"Do you happen to know an old man by the name of Abe Wilkins?" Riley asked.

The man pondered the question for a moment, then shook his head. "Don't recollect so, but the name sounds familiar."

Riley thanked him and headed toward the boardinghouse. His mouth watered for a good hot meal—anything but canned beans and salt pork. A whole pot of decent coffee sounded tempting too. He opened the door and stepped inside. Immediately the sound of angry voices met his ears.

"I'm telling you the corn bread is harder than rocks. How do you expect the customers to eat it? Use a hammer? Blow it apart with a shotgun?"

"There's nothing wrong with my corn bread," a woman said. The clanging of pans punctuated her opinion of the man's criticism. "You didn't use to complain about my cooking."

"I didn't have a choice then. Now, I can do better myself." The man stepped into view, and Riley recognized him as an old drinking partner by the name of Roy. Startled, the man blinked, then ushered Riley to a chair. "Excuse me, that's my wife," he said. "Hilda, Darlin', we have a customer." His voice inched louder.

"I don't care if we do. You insulted my cooking."

Roy turned to Riley. "Take my advice and stay clear of the corn bread. It'll break your teeth."

"What did you say?" Hilda, a right muscular woman, stood just behind them.

"Uh, nothing. I asked if he wanted something sweet."

Hilda's gaze shot fire. "I heard every word you said." She picked up two pieces of the corn bread and threw them at her husband. He ducked, and so did Riley. The bread hit the wall with a dull thud. When Hilda saw they hadn't reached their target, she threw two more.

Riley knew he didn't need to get in the middle of any marital squabble. Best he leave and eat his own cooking.

"I'll fix you," Hilda said, chasing Roy around the room.

In that split instant, Riley saw a cast-iron skillet head his way. He moved but not fast enough. The skillet hit the side of his head. Stunned, he headed for the door before the woman killed him. Riley's head exploded into a thunderous roar. Dazed, he stumbled out of the building and down the street toward the livery stable. Maybe he could pay the owner there for a meal.

"Riley O'Connor, what are you doing in Mesquite?" Judge Balsh asked from across the street. "I told you never to come back with your drinking and fighting, and here you are drunk."

"I'm not drunk, Judge," Riley said, holding his head. "The folks at the boardinghouse were having an argument, and I got stuck in the middle of it."

"I could round up a kid who could lie better than that. I've had a bad day, and now you show up. I told you before that I'd send you to prison if I ever saw you in Mesquite again, and I always keep my word." The judge glanced down the street to the jail. "O'Connor, you are under arrest."

three

A commotion outside the jail startled Nettie. She'd been praying about her dilemma and her conversation with Maudie Mae when Judge Balsh's booming voice seized her attention.

"Don't be arguing with me. I told you four years ago what would happen if you set foot in this town again."

"Judge, I intended to be here but a few hours, long enough for provisions and to find a man I owe a debt."

Nettie strained her ears and stood up from the filthy cot. The voice echoed from somewhere in the past.

"Truth known, you owe a lot of people in Mesquite."

The judge sounded more riled than he'd been at her arrest. If this man made the judge that mad, would he make her stay in jail a little longer? Nettie glanced at Sheriff Kroft. He slammed shut his dime novel and jumped to his feet. His thumbs hooked on either side of his gun belt.

"You don't scare anybody." Nettie lifted her chin. "Are you imitating one of the heroes in your book?"

"Hush, Miss Nettie. I have a job to do."

"You mean following the judge's orders every time he barks?"

The sheriff tossed her a frustrated glance, but before he could reply, the jail door opened, and Judge Balsh escorted Riley O'Connor inside.

Riley O'Connor? What is he doing here? The last Nettie heard, Riley had left Archerville to parts unknown. How disgusting! In all her dealings with people, he stood out as the most despicable of them all. Back in Archerville, Riley had pestered the daylights out of her dear friend Lena even after she married Gabe. Nettie remembered birthing Lena's two little girls—the prettiest babies in Nebraska.

The judge shouted at the sheriff and once again captured Nettie's attention. "Lock him up, Sheriff. I'll figure out what to do with him in a couple of days."

"Judge, please listen to me. If you'd talk to the man at the boardinghouse, he'd back up my story," Riley said.

"All I know is you're drunk and you're in Mesquite. Nothing else matters right now."

Riley whipped his attention to the sheriff. "Would you check out my story, Sheriff? I promise you I'm telling the truth."

A huge red knot rose on Riley's forehead, the same side as an ugly scar from below his eye to nearly his jaw. How did he get that? It sure marred Riley's handsome face. Of course, Nettie had never paid him any attention. No good Christian woman would ever look twice at a no-account like Riley O'Connor. She simply remembered what other women had said.

Shaking her head to dispel some of the memories about Riley, Nettie stole a look at his eyes. They were the most incredible deep blue she'd ever seen—reminding her of a cloudless sky at high noon. For a moment she thought. . .no, couldn't be. Impossible.

Riley must have sensed her scrutiny, because he met her gaze. Instantly she whirled around in the cell. Thoroughly humiliated, Nettie felt the heat rise from her bosom to her neck and face. Maybe he didn't recognize her, especially if he had partaken of alcohol. She patted the severely styled bun at her nape. Once assured not a single hair had strayed, she squared her shoulders and took her previous seat on the wretched cot.

"Sure glad we have two cells," Sheriff Kroft said. "Our other prisoner might not take too kindly to sharing her quarters with a man." He gave Riley a gentle push inside the cell adjoining Nettie's.

She refused to give the men any attention. Soon she'd be out. She had to believe God would direct the judge to let her go.

A deep belly laugh from Judge Balsh echoed around the small jail. The muscular man shook with amusement about something. "This is the best thing that's happened all day. Don't you see?" he asked the sheriff between guffaws.

"Naw, not really."

"First, Nettie's here because of stomping into my saloon and disturbing my customers with her notions about drinking, then O'Connor shows up drunk after I told him to never come back to town."

"Oh yeah." The sheriff slapped his hand against his thigh. He released a high-pitched heehaw, sounding more like an aggravated mule than a laughing man. "Makes for a real interesting day, doesn't it?"

"Sure does." The judge peered at Nettie. "You've got your work cut out for you, Miss Nettie. I suggest you start praying for this man's soul, 'cause he's the worst of his kind."

"Judge," Riley began.

"Keep quiet. I'll hear your case in three days. That'll give me time to research what I can charge you with before sending you to prison." With those words, Judge Balsh whirled around to the sheriff. "You keep your eyes on both of them. If either one of them escapes, I'll have your badge."

The sheriff gulped. "Yes, Sir. I mean, yes, Judge. Those two aren't going anywhere."

"Judge," Nettie called, standing again and grasping the metal bars. "When are you letting me out of here?"

"Never." The judge's voice rose to thunder level. "You've ruined my day once too often." He shook his finger in the sheriff's face. "Don't you dare let my wife in here. Understand?"

"Yes, Judge." The sheriff's Adam's apple bobbled like an apple in a barrel of water.

"Maybe I'll get lucky and they will kill each other," the judge said as he stormed through the jail door. Then he laughed. "I know exactly what I'll put on their tombstones: Riley O'Connor, drunk up to his collar, and Nettie Franklin, despised drinking men."

The door slammed behind him, shaking the entire jail. Nettie blinked back the tears. *Oh, dear, what would happen now?*

ىۈ

Riley thought maybe he had this coming. Riding into Mesquite today after the way he'd left years ago wasn't real smart, but Nettie Franklin? From what he remembered, she'd been a rather quiet woman, never caused trouble. His pain-glazed brain kicked in, and he recalled her being a midwife. He'd always thought she had a pretty face—shiny, raven-colored hair, pink-tinted cheeks as though she might burst into a full blush, and gray eyes shaped like half moons. She should have married and mothered a whole basketful of kids by now.

"Miss Nettie," Riley said, "I don't think it was proper for the judge to poke fun at you. I'm sorry."

Her mouth dropped open.

"Excuse me." Riley removed his hat. "Do you remember me from Archerville?"

Nettie nodded. "I. . .are you drunk?"

Obviously his reputation had not been forgotten. "No, Ma'am. I haven't had a drink in over four years."

She closed her mouth, but her eyes widened.

"I've changed, Miss Nettie. I'm not the wild heathen you once knew." How he wanted her to see the truth in him.

Slowly she regained her composure, smoothed her skirt, then folded her hands in front of her. "You do talk differently."

"Yes, Ma'am. I became a Christian when I quit drinking."

"Praise God." A smile spread over her face. For a moment Riley believed he'd looked into the face of an angel. Surely not, for Nettie Franklin stood before him. "I'm very happy for you."

"God had to hit me square in the heart for me to listen," Riley said, "but I finally understood."

"I find that a bit impossible to believe, Riley," Sheriff Kroft said. "Even I have a hard time following the Lord, and I ain't never done all you have."

Riley appreciated the sheriff's honesty. "It's not so hard when you figure out who's the boss."

The sheriff shook his head. "Don't expect the judge to believe all that."

"Yeah, but it's the truth. Would you do me a favor and stop by the boardinghouse? I walked in when the two were in the middle of an argument. I dodged a few pieces of the wife's corn bread, but I didn't duck in time when she sent a skillet across the room. I know Roy will back up my story, unless Hilda knocked him out."

The sheriff studied him for a moment. "Guess I could. Most folks know those two fight worse than a pair of roosters. And I ain't smellin' no whiskey on you."

"Thank you," Riley said. "All I wanted was a hot meal."

The sheriff chuckled. "Well, you won't get it there. The food's worse than mine." With those words, he sat back at his desk, propped up his feet, and pulled out his book.

Riley turned his attention back to Nettie. "How long have you been in Mesquite?"

She hesitated before answering. "About three years. I came to teach school."

"Like I said, a good lady like yourself shouldn't be in jail. I'm sure the judge will have you out soon."

Nettie sighed, and her thin shoulders rose and fell like the petals of a wildflower caught on the wind. "You sure don't sound like the Riley O'Connor I knew in Archerville."

"I'm not the same man, and I intend to make amends to the folks I've wronged." He rubbed his callused fingers over the worn brim of his hat. "I know what you're thinking, and I wrote

Lena and Gabe a letter about three years ago apologizing for my past actions." He felt her lingering gaze and braved forward. "If you want, I'll be glad to listen to how you got here. Sounds like you got on the wrong side of the judge."

"I did, indeed." She proceeded to tell Riley about her call to the temperance movement and what happened at the judge's saloon.

"Maybe a different approach might have been better." He hoped she could sense his sincerity.

Nettie crossed her arms over her chest and stamped her foot. "How dare you doubt a call from God?"

He'd upset her good. "Miss Nettie, I don't doubt your call for one minute. No, Ma'am, not at all. But I can't help but ask myself if God told you to grab that man's drink and pour it on the floor."

If a woman's gaze could set a man on fire, Riley would be roasting over a roaring blaze. "Are you saying I'm not close enough to our Lord to heed His commands?"

Riley held up his hands in defense. "No, Ma'am. I'm simply making an observation."

"Don't bother. Riley O'Connor, I believe you're still a heathen."

❧

Hours later, when the sun had gone down and the only light came from a candle on the deputy's desk, Nettie wept softly in the dark shadows. Never had she felt so alone and misunderstood. The judge despised her. Her best friend questioned her actions, and no one else in town had been to visit. The fact that Riley O'Connor snored in the next cell didn't help either. Earlier today, she'd debated whether her actions had been orchestrated by God. Riley had asked her the same thing. Doubts mingled with misery moved her to shed one tear after another.

At this very moment, she'd be tempted to do just about anything to get out of jail. A light rap at the door gave her a new spring of hope. Perhaps the judge had ordered her release. Slowly the door swung open, and Maudie Mae bustled in.

"Mrs. Balsh," the deputy said. The young man had been nearly asleep. Obviously he hadn't heeded the sheriff's orders to keep alert.

"Yes, Deputy, what do you need?"

The young man stumbled over his words. "I thought you wanted me."

"Just your keys." Maudie Mae clicked her fingers.

The deputy shook his head. "No, Ma'am. Sheriff Kroft gave me orders to not let you in."

"Well, I'm here, and since I'm already inside this fine establishment, why not unlock Miss Nettie's cell so I can give her a decent supper?"

"Can't, Ma'am. The judge and the sheriff would string me up."

Maudie Mae hurried past the deputy and lifted the key from the desktop. "Then I'll do it myself."

Nettie wished she could see her friend's face, but Maudie Mae's back was turned to her.

"I cannot allow you to interfere with the law," the deputy said.

Maudie Mae walked toward Nettie's cell. "Then don't look. If I thought for one minute you had a real criminal here, I'd be the first to back you. But this woman is not guilty of anything but following her heart."

In the next instant, her friend sat with her on the cot. Nettie smelled pork chops and greens, and her stomach growled. The boardinghouse owner had brought two plates of stew for her and Riley, but it tasted of shoe leather.

"What did the judge say?" Nettie asked. "I can't bear to be in here another hour."

Maudie Mae grasped Nettie's hand. "The judge is meeting with the sheriff, so I can't stay long. What I wanted to tell you is I've talked to the judge about your release."

"And? Tell me, please."

"He says he's thinking on it. But I've been pondering over it too, and we might have a way out of here yet."

Nettie felt her insides churn.

"He'll release you to a family member who will accept full responsibility for all of your actions."

She burst into tears. "But I don't have any family here in Mesquite." The panic she'd experienced earlier now wrapped its icy fingers around her heart.

"I know." Maudie Mae patted her hand like her mother used to do. "That's what I've been thinking about—how to get around the judge's mandate."

Confused, Nettie needed to hear Maudie Mae's plan. It all sounded, well, immoral and definitely against God's principles. "We can't make up a family, Maudie Mae. It's a sin for sure."

"But I know a couple who, for a small amount of money, would state you're an aunt."

Nettie covered her face. "Listen to what you're saying. It's pure deceit."

Her friend nodded. "You're right. God forgive me, Nettie, I really want to help you get out of here."

"Is there no other way?" Nettie knew she'd be sobbing in the next breath. The idea of falling asleep on the dirty cot made her wonder what varmints would crawl out of the straw mattress and bite her.

"I'll pay a visit to the preacher. I'm sure he can talk to the judge."

"Good." Nettie's hopes lifted a mite.

"But I can't until tomorrow."

"Not till then?" Nettie thought her heart might give out for good.

"The judge will have a fit if he comes home and I'm gone. You know how angry he can get."

Misery inched its way through her body. Suddenly she

itched, and something darted across the floor. Nettie screamed, and she heard Riley and the deputy rush to her cell.

"What's wrong?" the deputy asked.

"I think I saw a mouse." Nettie's attention darted in every direction.

The deputy laughed. "They won't bother you. I hear them scurrying about 'most every night."

Nettie turned to Maudie Mae. "Any more suggestions before I go insane?"

"Actually, I have. We could find you a husband."

four

Riley exploded into laughter. Never had he listened to two women discuss a problem and how to solve it. Perhaps he should have ignored their conversation, but when the judge's wife burst through the door and wakened him, his curiosity got the best of him. Poor Nettie. Right from the beginning he'd felt sorry for her plight. She might have been a bit misguided and in his opinion stretched her calling a bit, but she didn't deserve jail. Judge Balsh took his anger out on her, and most likely Riley showing up in town had a lot to do with it.

"Riley O'Connor, you have no right to make fun of me," Nettie said. "Now, you stop your laughing this very minute. This is serious. You just go on back to sleep and mind your own business."

"A husband, Miss Nettie? How are you going to get a husband while you're in jail?"

Maudie Mae reached for Nettie's hand. "Don't you worry about a thing."

"But I don't want a husband," Nettie said. "I just want out of here so I can go home."

"I know, Dear. We'll think of something." Maudie Mae rose to her feet. "I have to go now before the judge returns home."

"I understand." Nettie hiccupped. "Do you think I'll be released later on tonight?"

Maudie Mae hesitated. "Probably not. But I'll be back in the morning. Try your best to get some sleep."

Long after the judge's wife left, Nettie's soft weeping brought compassion to Riley's heart. "I'm sorry, Miss Nettie. I didn't mean to hurt your feelings. I'm sure the judge will change his mind. Why don't you try to get some rest like Miss Maudie Mae suggested?"

"I don't think I can." She sobbed. "The cot is so dirty, and I'm afraid of mice."

The deputy's feet hit the floor. "If you aren't comfortable in Mesquite's jail, then don't break the law."

Riley didn't comment. He'd probably make things worse. *Lord, I may not agree with what Miss Nettie did, but a lady shouldn't be in jail. Would You help her? Thanks—and Lord, would You get me out of here too? I'll never bother the judge's town again. I promise.*

The following morning, the preacher visited. He introduced himself to Riley as James Faulkner, then listened to Miss Nettie's sad tale. Unfortunately Preacher Faulkner offered little sympathy.

"Miss Nettie, pointing fingers and making accusations will never win over the souls of sinners," he said. "You've made Judge Balsh angry, and unlike our Lord, he doesn't have a forgiving nature."

"What do you suggest?" She paced the cell. "Certainly you don't condone drinking."

A muscle twitched on the preacher's portly cheek. "Of course not." He paused, and his voice softened. "Miss Nettie, our Lord wants us to love the sinner into His kingdom. Most folks know when they've done wrong, and most folks want to change. They need to see a difference in the lives of believers before they see their own ways are not the best."

Nettie stiffened. She folded her hands primly in her lap. "How could I have handled the situation differently?"

"You could have introduced yourself to the bartender, said you were a member of Mesquite's Gospel Church, and invited them to come to one of our services," the preacher said.

She stared at the floor.

"If those folks were really burdened with the sin in their lives, they'd learn about it in church."

Riley whispered "amen" under his breath. Preacher Faulkner had shared a good bit of wisdom from under that black hat.

Nettie sat on the cot beside the preacher. "Some of us ladies sang hymns outside the saloon and even passed out information about the evils of drinking, but none of the saloon's customers ever showed up on Sundays."

"I'm glad to hear you're working for the Lord." He glanced up at Riley in the next cell and offered a thin-lipped smile. "Have you ever considered bringing a hot meal to the ladies working there or seeing if any of them are sick? Maybe a couple of the ladies could visit the jail and see who's been locked up." The moment he uttered those words, he turned red. "I'm sorry; I meant for being drunk and disorderly."

"That's all right, and no, Preacher Faulkner, I haven't done any of those things." Nettie blinked back a tear.

He nodded. "Well, it's something to consider. I've been told you're a mighty fine cook, Miss Nettie. Those folks need people to show the church cares about them."

"I understand," Nettie said. "I may not agree with everything you said, but I certainly see your viewpoint."

"Good." Preacher Faulkner smiled. "I'll talk to the judge about your release."

"Thank you so much," Nettie replied. "Is there anything I can do to help matters?"

"I suggest you ask the sheriff or deputy for paper and write a letter of apology."

Nettie gasped. "I'll consider your suggestions, but I believe you're wrong."

"How badly do you want to get out of here?"

Nettie didn't reply.

Preacher Faulkner said a word of prayer to strengthen Nettie during her hardship and promised to stop by the following day.

"May I have a word with you?" Riley asked the man the moment the preacher finished with Nettie.

"Most assuredly." Preacher Faulkner beamed. "Would you like for me to step over there?"

Riley suppressed a laugh at the pleased look on the preacher's face. "No, it's not necessary. I'm a believer, Sir. But this wasn't always the case."

Preacher Faulkner waved away Riley's statement. "The sheriff told me your story. Most admirable. A true work of God. He also expounded on why you're in jail."

"I see. My concern is not about my current situation, although it needs some divine intervention, but about a matter from the past."

"Oh?" Preacher Faulkner raised a brow.

"An old man from Mesquite doctored me one night after I got drunk and into a fight. He gave me a Bible. His name is Abe Wilkins. I thought you might know him."

The preacher rubbed his jaw. "I saw Abe about six months ago when he stopped in for a visit. He had a little extra money and wanted it given to the poor. Abe lives alone about twenty miles outside of town. Good man. God fearing. What do you need him for, Son?"

"To thank him. If it hadn't been for Abe Wilkins, I'd have probably died in the street and be stoking eternal fire today." Riley felt joy coming from his heart. "I'd like for him to know his work paid off."

Preacher Faulkner glanced at Nettie. "See, Miss Nettie, that's exactly what I'm talking about—being Jesus to those who need Him."

Nettie looked away and said nothing.

❧

On the second and third days, Preacher Faulkner visited the jail. He appeared to enjoy Riley's company more than Nettie's. The very thought of a preacher preferring Riley O'Connor to her infuriated Nettie.

To make matters worse, the judge refused to overturn his

decision or set a date to hear Nettie's and Riley's cases. He accepted the boardinghouse owner's word about how Riley obtained the gash to his head, but the fact remained the judge had ordered Riley to never come back to Mesquite.

By the morning of the fifth day, Nettie no longer feared she'd go insane, she already had. Sleepless nights. Long hot days. The food from the boardinghouse tasted like dirt. She needed a bath, and she'd had enough of Sheriff Kroft or the deputy escorting her to the outhouse. How much humiliation could one woman take?

Lord, this is powerful bad. Is this in Your plan for me? And Lord, I don't agree with Preacher Faulkner Those folks inside the saloon are too hardheaded to come to church. I haven't forgotten how Jesus handled the moneychangers in the temple.

Maudie Mae had been by every day without a single word of good news. "The ladies in the Bible study are all praying for you," she said. "The judge will give in any time now. Just pray and have faith."

"I thought I was a strong woman, Maudie Mae. I believe in suffering for my faith and in speaking out despite persecution. I believe in dying for the Lord and in following Him with a pure heart. I want to do what I'm supposed to, but I can't stand one more day in this jail."

"What does Preacher Faulkner think about all this?"

Nettie gritted her teeth. "He suggested writing a letter to the judge."

"Splendid."

"I already gave the letter to Preacher Faulkner."

"And? The judge didn't say anything about it to me."

"He found it amusing."

"What did you say?" Maudie Mae asked.

"I apologized for disturbing the peace and gave him some Scripture verses about drunkenness."

Maudie Mae moaned and shook her head.

Strangely enough, the only good part about being in jail came from Riley's company. The man had found his salvation, and the two spent long hours discussing various aspects of the Bible. She steered away from how God felt about drinking for fear the judge might find out she hadn't curbed her tongue.

If Nettie hadn't been in jail, she wouldn't have spent her time talking to Riley. He'd done some powerfully bad things in Archerville and in Mesquite. Frankly, she'd have feared damage to her reputation. Schoolteachers were under constant, intensive scrutiny.

A lump formed in Nettie's stomach. She hadn't considered this aspect of her future before. All this time sitting in jail, she'd been thinking about school in the fall and how much she missed the children. If and when the judge ever let her go, she might not have a job. She feared all of her dreams of teaching precious children might have vanished when she walked into the judge's saloon. Her attempt to convert folks who had no intentions of changing their evil ways had led her into this cell.

Nettie loved children, which was one reason why she'd become a midwife and later taught school. Hopes of ever bearing her own babies disappeared when no decent man proposed marriage. A few had asked, but something about all of them bothered her. Nettie shrugged her shoulders and stepped to the metal bars. Her stomach growled, although she'd attempted breakfast. The scrambled eggs lacked salt, the bacon was black as embers, and she found it impossible to bite down on the corn bread. And the coffee. . .well, a proper lady dare not make such analogies. The deputy's words echoed in her mind every time she thought of complaining: *"If you aren't comfortable in Mesquite's jail, then don't break the law."*

Late that afternoon, Maudie Mae arrived with a basket of food. Nettie smelled it the moment her friend opened the door. A bit of heaven had entered Mesquite's jail.

Maudie Mae rummaged through the mound of food. "I

have fried chicken, corn, tender greens, corn bread, and gooseberry pie for Nettie and Riley. Oh, yes, and fresh buttermilk too."

"I've died and joined the Lord's banquet table," Riley said, rubbing his stomach. "I hope the judge appreciates you."

"Humph, that remains to be seen," Maudie Mae said. She glanced at Sheriff Kroft. "What are you gawking at?"

"You did bring me something, didn't you, Mrs. Balsh? I've been letting you visit Miss Nettie and all."

Maudie Mae frowned, then waved her hand at him. "Of course I did. You're the best sheriff this town ever had."

Nettie let a soft moan escape her lips. "You're an angel of mercy." She almost cried, but lately she'd shed enough tears to last a lifetime.

After a fine feast, Maudie Mae devoted her time to Nettie. She planted her bony body onto the cot and patted the remaining space beside her. "Sit down. We need to talk."

Nettie's heart thundered in her brain. "What's happened?"

"Just hear me out first." When Nettie obeyed, the woman took a deep breath. "The judge isn't about to change his mind soon—at least not for the next month. I've done some asking around town, and no one is willing to marry you—"

"Maudie Mae!"

"Hush. Let me finish."

"All right, but I don't like the way this is headed."

"I've done some researching, and I found out a man and woman can get married and then have it annulled by the judge within a few days."

Nettie rubbed her face, noting her fingers smelled of fried chicken. "What are you saying?"

Maudie Mae peered over at Riley, who rested on his cot. "If you and Riley married, both of you could leave this jail. According to the law, the judge would annul the marriage in a few days. This means Riley here could ride out of town, and you could go back to your life." She smiled, obviously thrilled with her plan. She leaned over to whisper, "He's a comely man, even with that scar. Have you noticed his blue eyes?"

Nettie shivered. She thought of screaming. Yes, she'd noticed Riley's eyes, and his auburn hair that reminded her of a sunset, and the times he talked real polite. He'd been clean-shaven when she knew him before, but the jail didn't provide a razor.

Even so, marrying for the sake of getting out of jail? Look what he'd done to her dear friend in Archerville. How did God feel about such a scheme?

"There's nothing wrong with what I'm proposing," Maudie Mae said. "It's not as though. . .well, you know what I mean."

The heat rose in Nettie's face, and her stomach felt like she'd hatched butterflies. "I–I don't think I can do what you're asking. Something about it seems very wrong."

"Well, let's see what Mr. O'Connor has to say about the idea. Mr. O'Connor, are you awake?"

Mortified, Nettie attempted to stop Maudie Mae, but the woman blurted her idea to Riley in one quick breath.

He stared at Maudie Mae as though she'd swallowed a mule. "That's about the craziest idea I've ever heard."

"Well, you're looking at heading to prison if you don't." She turned to Nettie, then back to Riley. "Think about this, you two. The judge would be rid of Riley, and Nettie's too scared to ever attempt any foolishness again."

Riley nodded and stood from his cot.

"Are you agreeing to this?" Alarm rang in Nettie's mind.

"I'm thinking on it," he replied. "I need to find Abe Wilkins and get back to my ranch in Montana. As long as Maudie Mae says it's legal."

Maudie Mae gave a quick nod. "Of course it's according to the law. So shall I talk to the judge?"

"Absolutely not." Nettie crossed her arms over her chest. "I'll rot in here before I marry Riley."

Maudie Mae eyed her up and down. "Have you taken a look at yourself lately? My nose tells me you don't have far to go."

Covering her face, Nettie didn't know whether to cry or pound her fist into the wall. *Lord, I have to get out of here, and I don't see any other way out.* What Maudie Mae suggested wasn't illegal or immoral as long as she and Riley didn't intend to *act* married. She had no future in jail, no way to do God's work or even perform any of the acts of kindness that preacher Faulkner spoke about. She lifted her gaze to Riley. "What do you think?"

ða

Riley watched the varied moods on Nettie's face—a pretty face, although right now her cheeks were smudged and her hair looked like the grease Mrs. Balsh fried the chicken in. Dark circles beneath her eyes were big enough to bury a prairie dog, and he felt sorry for her because of all the crying she'd done.

Rubbing his whiskered jaw, Riley realized he had no room to criticize. He'd needed a bath before the judge threw him in jail. Even his horse smelled better. Inhaling deeply, he thought about all the work waiting for him at the ranch— and all the things he wanted to say to Abe Wilkins. Guess this arrangement might suit them all.

five

Judge Balsh gave his blessings to Riley and Nettie's wedding. In fact, he visited the jail to tell them so.

"Riley, you're willing to take responsibility for this woman?" he asked. When Riley agreed, he turned to Nettie. "And you're willing to take responsibility for this drunk?"

Nettie wanted to state Riley didn't partake of strong drink anymore, but feared upsetting the judge. "Yes, I will."

The judge chuckled before breaking into a long round of laughter. He sobered and pointed a finger first at Riley and then at Nettie. "You two best understand that if either of you cross me wrong, you're both in jail."

"Yes, Sir," Riley said. "I have a ranch to run in Montana, and I'll never set foot in this town again."

"And I'll never set foot inside your saloon again," Nettie said.

The judge frowned. "What about leading Maudie Mae astray with your temperance talk?"

Nettie's knees began to tremble. "I'll. . .I'll talk of other things with her, other ways to persuade folks not to drink."

"Good." The judge smiled. "Shall I perform the honors?"

"Ah, I'd like Preacher Faulkner to marry us," Riley said before Nettie could utter a word. She guessed he wanted to make sure things were done proper.

Later she talked to Maudie Mae about the situation. Nettie's insides twisted and turned with the idea of marrying Riley.

"You have to do this," Maudie Mae said. "But don't tell Preacher Faulkner about our plan. He might not think too highly of us."

"I'm wondering how God feels about all this," Nettie said.

Every time she considered duping the preacher and the judge who had sent her to jail, a throbbing headache took over her senses. "And what about my position as schoolteacher? How is the school board going to react to a marriage annulment?"

Maudie Mae tossed her an irritated glance. "Tend to one problem at a time. First let's get you married so you can get out of jail."

Nettie sighed heavily and glanced at Riley, who had heard every word. "What do you think, Riley? Are we committing a sin by getting married for a few days?"

Riley stood up from his cot and stared at her thoughtfully. "I'm thinking if there's a difference between what the law says and what God says. I don't remember ever reading where God said a marriage in name only was against His ways."

"See," Maudie Mae said. "Let's get both of you out of here, and then you can deal with the particulars."

Nettie started to ask what kind of particulars but changed her mind when the familiar mouse ran across the jail floor. She'd do about anything to get out of jail.

Preacher Faulkner performed the wedding ceremony with Maudie Mae and the sheriff as witnesses. No one offered to tell the preacher the real reason why Riley and Nettie desired marriage. The preacher seemed pleased as a little boy with a handful of sugar cookies.

During the ceremony, Nettie could not keep her mind on the preacher's words. The hope of getting married had faded as the years passed her by, but when she had entertained the thought, it hadn't been under circumstances like this. Back then, she'd wanted a church wedding with flowers and friends. She'd dreamed of a beautiful dress, a new one she'd make just for the occasion and later wear to church. Most importantly, she'd lived her whole life waiting for a wonderful man who'd love her as Jesus loved the Church.

Nettie glanced at Riley. He smelled as badly as she. And

her dress was filthy. When she took it off, it would stand by itself. How could God be in this? Up until a few days ago, her recollection of Riley had been powerful bad. Now, she stood there with a wall separating them, listening to Preacher Faulkner pronouncing them man and wife.

I want to get this done so I can go home. Nettie prayed the school board would not dismiss her. Without the children, she had little meaning in her life. Without a job, she had no visible means to support herself, another problem to add to her ever-growing mound of troubles.

❧

Riley felt sorry for the woman on the other side of the wall. He heard a muffled sob and knew her tears weren't any semblance of happiness. A woman had special dreams about her wedding day, and he was certain this moment lent itself to more of a nightmare than a blessed event.

Riley didn't understand why a comely woman like Nettie Franklin had never gotten married in the first place. He liked her show of intelligence and the way she had special insight into the Bible. She did have a few strange ideas about how to get folks to stop drinking, but Riley wasn't discounting the fact she made sense. Alcohol sent a lot of good men and women on a path to ruin, and he'd been one of them. Nettie's methods might not be the best, but she had a pure heart about helping people.

When another sob met his ears, Riley wished he could put his arms around her. Nettie deserved better than this. He'd heard her speak about the children at her school, and whether she wanted to admit it or not, he doubted she still had a teaching position.

A gnawing in his gut told him Maudie Mae's scheme didn't set well with the Lord. He should have spoken up sooner about it and trusted God to get them out of jail. The more he considered the plan, the more he realized the Lord did have some pretty strong words about deceiving. Take Jacob, for example.

Look what deceiving his father had cost him. Jacob spent years away from his family for fear his brother would kill him. As a result, others deceived him, and the problems just got worse.

Riley had to say something. The urgency in his spirit refused to rest. He cleared his throat, but the words stayed fixed in his mind.

"And so by the power vested in me, I now pronounce you man and wife."

Oh Lord, what have I done?

As soon as the ceremony ended, the sheriff produced the papers Judge Balsh requested Riley and Nettie sign, making them responsible for each other. Riley thanked Preacher Faulkner and told him he'd be paying for the preacher's services as soon as he got his horse at the livery.

"You two have some time together before you concern yourself about financial matters," Preacher Faulkner said. "I'll be at the church or the parsonage, and I haven't forgotten you wanted to visit with Abe Wilkins."

"Thank you," Riley said and shook the man's hand. He intended to find Abe before he left for Montana. After spending the last few days in jail, Riley was more determined to at least find the man who'd influenced his decision to know the Lord.

Nettie and Riley stepped out into the fresh air with Maudie Mae looking as pleased as a cat who just swallowed a mouse—maybe the one that scurried across the cell floors. Riley took in the July sunshine and believed the light and warmth were the finest he'd ever known. All he needed now to make his joy complete would be to ride out of Mesquite in a day or so with this marriage and his past behind him. He stole a peek at Nettie, who acted as though she'd already died and mingled with the angels.

"I never thought the sky could look so blue," she said. "I wonder if folks really appreciate its beauty."

"I doubt it," Riley said. "We're all guilty of taking things for granted."

The threesome stood in the middle of the street, while Riley contemplated what to do next. Whatever did you say to a woman whom you just married, but really didn't?

"I guess I'll go see about my horse," he finally said, "then pay the preacher."

"Do I owe you anything?" She wrung her hands in her familiar nervous manner.

Riley shook his head. "No, Ma'am. I'm taking care of it."

"Thank you," she said, avoiding his scrutiny. "I guess I'll be heading home."

"Do you need a ride? I could take you on my horse." Riley shifted nervously.

"Oh no," Nettie said, her attention drawn to a couple of pigs passing by. "I have my mule and wagon."

"Nonsense," Maudie Mae interrupted. "Newlyweds should be seen together." She shooed Riley away like an old woman scattering chickens from her garden. "You walk to the livery together, then leave town in the direction of Nettie's home. That'll look good."

Mortified, Nettie reddened and looked down the street at absolutely nothing.

"When do we see the judge about this other issue?" Riley asked. He hated to bring up the annulment with the ink still wet on their wedding and responsibility papers, but he had things to do.

Maudie Mae hooked Nettie's arm into Riley's. "Day after tomorrow," she said. "Don't want to make anything look suspicious. I'll meet you right here in front of the jailhouse on Thursday morning at ten o'clock." She smiled as though satisfied, then disappeared toward her home on the opposite end from the livery.

Riley patted Nettie's hand. "I'm powerful sorry about all this."

"Me too," she said. Her voice sounded like a squeak. "I feel like we made light of God's sacred view of marriage."

Riley groaned. "I should have said what I really felt about Maudie Mae's plan. But I didn't see any other way out of jail."

Only the sounds of a barking dog irritating a couple of squealing pigs intruded on the silence that prevailed between them.

"Don't shelter all the blame," Nettie said at last. "I didn't refuse either. All I could think about was that horrible cell."

"And I wanted to find Abe Wilkins and get back to my ranch more than trusting God to get us out of there."

Nettie sniffed, then lifted her head. "We did something very bad back there, Riley O'Connor. I'm not too proud to say I'm afraid."

"I feel the same way."

"I'm asking God to forgive me and show me how to make it up to Him."

Riley wondered if again he should say what he felt, especially since the last time he didn't stand up for God, he'd ended up getting married. "We can't make it up to God, Nettie," he said as gently as he knew how. "I don't know the verse word for word, but in Ephesians it says we're saved by grace, not by anything we do. Forgiveness is a gift from God."

She lifted her gray gaze to him, trusting-like, in a way that made Riley feel like a godly man. Given another circumstance, he'd have thanked God for this opportunity to be used by Him. But this situation didn't pat anyone on the back.

"You're right," she said. "I guess this time next week, all of this will be over. You'll be heading back to Montana, and I'll be wondering if I still have a job."

He nodded. Hopefully, he'd feel better in a few days when the annulment separated him from Miss Nettie. Right now, he had to pretend love and devotion to the woman on his arm because, no pretending about it, she was the new Mrs. O'Connor.

❧

Nettie leafed through the pages of her well-worn Bible to Ephesians, from where Riley had earlier quoted those verses. His horse tracks were still visible in the dirt outside her soddie, and if she opened her door, she'd be able to see him in the distance, riding toward the outskirts of town.

"Where is it?" Impatience tugged at her senses. There in the second chapter of Ephesians, she read what Riley had spoken about: "For by grace are ye saved through faith; and that not of yourselves: it is the gift of God: Not of works, lest any man should boast."

Nettie well knew those words. Frustrated at herself and at Maudie Mae for dragging her into this situation, she closed the Bible and considered the seriousness of mocking God. She gulped. Unfortunately the goings-on today reminded her of Adam and Eve, not that Maudie Mae resembled a snake or Riley a piece of fruit. But what she and Riley had done was wrong, and she hated to think about God's discipline.

With a shake of her head, she whirled around in her small, two-room home. All her thoughts in jail had centered on coming home, taking a bath, and forgetting the temperance movement that ushered her there in the first place. Now, she had a horrible feeling all the bathwater in Nebraska wouldn't get her clean.

After heating several kettles of water, Nettie indulged in the long-awaited bath. Her hair squeaked clean beneath her fingertips, and although she felt horrible about the day, bathing helped. She allowed her mind to wander toward the end of summer when school commenced in Mesquite. The children were her delight. Since she'd never have any of her own, these precious ones easily wrapped her heart around their fingertips. They'd all have grown a foot and would be brown from playing and working outside.

A twinge of regret stole her fond thoughts. Surely the

school board wouldn't hold either her term in jail or her marriage against her. With a deep breath, she realized as strict as the rules were for schoolteachers, her teaching days were most likely over. Thinking otherwise made her look like a fool.

Temperance. God had called her to stand up against the use of alcohol. Hadn't He? Preacher Faulkner's words rolled around her mind. At the time, he'd angered her. Now she pondered his advice with a different perspective. Taking a deep breath, Nettie put herself in the shoes of one of those women who worked in the saloon. If someone burst into the saloon and declared her a sinner and spouted words of God, how would she feel?

A raw, aching feeling assaulted Nettie's stomach. She knew sometimes her stubborn and rebellious streak took over her senses, and she despised anyone telling her what to do, especially when they used authority. She much preferred a kind word being used to point out misgivings—like Riley had done today.

Maybe she could take a meal to those ladies and apologize for insulting them. She needed to make amends to the barkeeper, and as difficult as it would be, she must pay for Frank's drink. The thought of doing those things needled worse than a bee sting.

The following morning, Nettie slept long past sunup. Exhaustion had left her craving hour after hour of peaceful rest. By the time she put on a pot of coffee, the sun had nearly reached its peak. Before eating, she checked on her mule. The animal had received some kindly attention while she courted the jail. The poor chickens needed to be fed, and there were eggs to gather. Nettie even found a little tune inside her. Circumstances always had a way of working themselves out, and her trust must be in God to see things through.

Close to evening, Nettie sat outside with her needlework and noted a rider. As the figure drew closer, she recognized

Riley and waved. How nice of him to pay a visit. They had become friends, if one could associate finding lasting relationships with being in jail.

"How are you?" Nettie smiled as he pulled his chestnut mare close to her rocker.

"I've been better," he said.

Nettie's attention instantly flew to his face. The set of his jaw and the way he pressed his lips together alarmed her. "What's wrong?"

"Not so sure you want to hear this, but better from me than someone else."

He swung down from his horse, and Nettie noted his lanky frame. Sort of pleasing to look at. Suddenly apprehension gripped her.

"Riley, you best tell me real fast 'cause you're scaring me."

"And rightfully so."

Nettie felt the blood rush from her face.

"Maudie Mae found me at Preacher Faulkner's house this afternoon." Riley hesitated. "Seems like she made a mistake."

"What kind of mistake?" Nettie trembled and dropped her needlework.

"Judge Balsh is not about to annul our marriage. He says you and me are married for good."

six

Nettie clutched her hand to her heart. Her head spun, and if not for Riley, she'd have fallen on her face. God had judged them for their deception.

"Maudie Mae must have made an error," she said, once Riley had her seated in the rocker. "She said Judge Balsh would annul the marriage and we could go on with our lives. Maybe she didn't hear him right."

Riley pushed his hat back from his forehead and looped his fingers in his belt. "I thought about going to see him, but I didn't relish the idea of spending more time in jail. He's got us, Nettie. We're married."

She bit down hard on her lip to avoid any semblance of tears. Her mind raced with possible solutions, but nothing made any sense short of divorce, and she knew God despised that.

"We're stuck with each other," she said. "I'm really sorry."

Little lines etched around his eyes, and he didn't look the remotest bit happy. Thankfully she didn't see any anger. "Nettie, I don't have anything against you. In fact, I like you. You're pretty, and you know a lot about the Bible. My problem. . ." He cleared his throat. "My problem is I have a ranch in Montana."

"And I have children to teach."

Riley took in a deep breath. "I was about to get to your schoolteaching."

She felt the color leave her face. "What do you mean?"

"Maudie Mae said the judge talked to the schoolboard. They don't want a woman who's been in jail teaching their children."

"I can't go back to teaching?" This time she thought she'd really cry.

"I'm powerful sorry, Nettie. Seems like things keep getting worse."

She swallowed. Judge Balsh would not get the best of her. She still had her temperance movement, but—

"What about my house? It belongs to the schoolboard."

Riley nodded. "You can live here until they find a new teacher."

A twinge of anger flitted through her mind. "That was exceptionally nice of them."

"We need to talk about this. I did some thinkin' on it while riding out here."

She kept her sights glued to the ground. Reality had settled on her like the choking dust beneath her feet. Married to Riley. No job. No home. Life could not get much worse.

"You're right," she said. "Come on inside. I'll make some coffee." She arose from the rocker and blinked a few times to steady herself. Glancing up at Riley, she noted he'd taken a bath and put on clean clothes. He was a right handsome man, even with the scar. When Nettie considered how he received the mark, he looked even more appealing. She grappled for her senses. What was she thinking? Admiring Riley meant trouble.

"Thank you." Riley's blue eyes attached to her heart. She instantly shoved her response to him to a remote corner of forgotten memories. This would never do.

Once inside, the familiarity of making coffee in her own home eased the discomfort of her reactions to Riley. She focused on the conversations they'd held in jail and how easily she could talk to him. Odd, nothing today entered her mind to discuss with Riley.

"How much land is with this house?" Riley seated himself in a chair, his long, lanky frame looking very much out of place.

Nettie managed a smile. Riley had even shined his boots. Nice to think he'd done this for her, but she knew better. "I have one hundred and sixty acres. It's part of Judge Balsh's land. It was a homestead piece that a man lost in a poker game in the judge's saloon. I don't know what he thought a schoolteacher might do with so much land. Why do you ask?"

"I'm thinking about buying it."

"What for?"

Riley released a heavy sigh and peered into her face. "For my wife."

Speechless—not one of Nettie's normal characteristics— she could only stare back at him. "I don't need anyone to take care of me."

"That might have been true before you got married and lost your job teaching school." His voice rose a bit louder.

"I'm not really married. I didn't mean what I said." She clamped her hands on her waist.

"Oh yeah?" He lifted a brow. "Tell that to Judge Balsh. Tell that to Preacher Faulkner. And while you're at it, tell it to God."

"You don't have to shout," Nettie said. "I know what I did."

"We did."

How one man could raise his voice and not move a muscle on his face was beyond Nettie. Her father's face had always scrunched up and turned tomato red when he was angry. "I'm well aware of the circumstances." She lowered her voice and lifted her chin, passing a disapproving look on to Riley much like she did to her students.

"Good. Now that we understand each other, I'd like to make sure you're taken care of before I leave for Montana."

"And I," she swallowed hard, "don't need you to take care of me. I'm quite capable of supporting myself."

Riley stood to his full six-feet-two height. "I've seen how you take care of yourself."

Nettie's temper flared. "Who are you to talk?"

"My reason for being in jail was a misunderstanding. I didn't break the law."

She searched for a retort while her heart drummed against

her chest. She needed time to sort through her jumbled thoughts. Nettie had been taking care of herself for a long time, and she'd find a way to continue.

"I will need to think about it," she finally said.

"You can think all you want, but it won't change a thing. When I have a responsibility, I follow it through." He walked over to where the coffee had finished brewing and reached for a mug looped through a peg on the wall. He poured the hot brew and sat down.

"I could always go back to being a midwife," she said, more to herself than Riley. "Or go back to Archerville."

"Whatever you do, I suggest you leave the temperance business alone."

Nettie's insides flared like a flame catching hold of straw. "How dare you tell me what to do?"

"There you go again, getting mad about a suggestion. As your husband, I'm forbidding you to traipse into the saloon again and cause trouble. Don't forget, I signed as responsible for you, and I have no desire to head back to jail."

For a moment, Nettie had forgotten one of the stipulations of getting out of the judge's cell. "I'll do as the Lord leads."

"I believe Preacher Faulkner made a few comments along that line."

"What right did you have to listen in on our private conversation?"

"I would have to be deaf not to overhear." Riley snatched up his cup and headed for the door.

Nettie wanted to whirl him around and push him back into the chair. "Where do you think you're going?"

"To the dugout. I'm going to unsaddle my horse and draw some water."

"Why's that?"

Riley slowly turned to face Nettie. His placid look unnerved her—that and the way his rugged features made her heart skip. "I'm staying right here until we get all of this worked out. I'm tired of sleeping on hard ground or in a cell. After all, you are my wife, and I have every right to be here."

❧

Riley kicked the side of the dugout in an effort to calm down. Before accepting Jesus, he'd have made tracks to the nearest bottle of red-eye, then lunged into a fight, but now he must handle his anger in a manner pleasing to God. If that was possible.

Nettie made him angrier than he'd ever been in his life. All he wanted to do was take care of her proper, since she now held the title of Mrs. Riley O'Connor. No one would ever say he ran out on his wife and left her defenseless.

Riley moaned. He'd never contemplated marriage. Never. Women were nothing but trouble. They cramped a man's style and then tried to mold the male population into something they wanted. Riley's observations of females, Nettie included, cited them as sweet-talking, unpredictable, and manipulative, and they had opinions about every topic known to man. At least Nettie didn't whine.

As much as he wanted to ride out and leave Nebraska in a cloud of dust, Riley couldn't do it. His conscience promised to pick at him forever.

Riley unsaddled his mare, fed, watered, and groomed her, all the while thinking about Nettie. If his wife hadn't been so stubborn and quick to argue, she'd be tolerable. What happened to the gentle woman who had talked to him about the Bible? They'd shared other conversations too. Had she simply played up to him so he'd oblige Maudie Mae's plan? The notion of those two women conspiring against him made Riley even more furious.

By the time he led the mare into the fenced area, the cow needed milking. Riley searched through the shadowed dugout and found a makeshift milking stool and a bucket. He placed them outside in hopes the display of a yellow-orange sunset might soothe his anger.

He tied the cow to a fencepost and eased onto the milking stool. Every ping in the wooden bucket served as a reminder of Nettie's quick tongue. Riley attempted to recite Scripture in his head, convinced if he kept his mind occupied, he'd not ponder the demise of Mrs. Riley O'Connor.

Long after the sun went down, Riley still sat with the cow, remembering a verse from Proverbs: "It is better to dwell in the wilderness, than with a contentious and an angry woman."

❧

Nettie poured corn bread batter into an iron skillet and stirred up a few precious eggs in a bowl for supper. At first she intended to make only enough for herself, but when she saw Riley milking the cow, she relented.

"What am I going to do?" she asked. Since living by herself, she'd picked up the habit of holding conversations aloud. "I'm not ready to be a wife."

The ring of the word "wife" gave her a chill. Besides carrying Riley's name, other duties fell under the title of Mrs. Riley O'Connor. She felt her face flush warm, and she hastily glanced about to see if he had possibly slipped inside.

Of course she had nothing to worry about. Riley hadn't so much as kissed her. She shivered again. Riley said he was sick of sleeping on the hard ground and in a cell. The only place left. . .

Nettie gulped and shook her head. She remembered when her friend Lena back in Archerville married Gabe Hunters. They hadn't known each other when they wed, so Gabe slept in the dugout with the animals until the weather hit below zero, then he slept in front of the fire. Sometime during the winter, the two realized they loved each other and everything turned out fine.

"That was Lena and Gabe," Nettie said. Her old friends hadn't tried to deceive anyone.

For a moment she allowed herself to imagine Riley kissing her. Nettie touched her lips with her fingers. She'd never been embraced by a suitor or courted, for that matter. After caring for her elderly parents until they died, she'd passed by the marrying age. A few men who had selfish reasons had asked, but she had no intentions of marrying a man simply because he needed a woman to take care of him. Nettie shrugged. Some folks said she had a comely look about her, but those were old people and women. They didn't count. Riley had said she was pretty.

Now her name wove with a man's as one—as the Bible said. Forever she'd be known as married, not a spinster. She should be overjoyed. She should call this a blessing. But instead she felt sick inside, worse than being locked up in jail for disrupting the judge's saloon.

Nettie heard Riley's boots stomp outside the door. Her heart fluttered, and she trembled like an autumn leaf. How could she get hold of herself? Prayer? Yes, of course. God still listened, although she had disappointed Him. *Please, Lord, I've made some terrible mistakes the past few days. Please forgive me and help me to talk to Riley without saying things to upset him. I know this is just as much my fault as his.*

The door opened, and she breathed a ragged breath before turning to greet him. An easy smile creased Riley's face, a bit crooked, like a little boy she had last year in school. He carried the bucket of milk, and she stepped to take it.

"Thank. . .thank you for milking the cow," she said.

"You're welcome. I needed something to do." He shoved his hands in his pockets.

"I'm making corn bread and stirrin' up eggs," she said with a gesture toward the fireplace. "It's a bit warm to be cooking inside, but I guess I wasn't thinking clear."

Riley shifted. "It smells good."

"There's plenty for you."

"I appreciate it. Nettie." He hesitated. "I don't want us to argue. We need to talk about this sensibly and figure out what we can do."

She set the milk down and wiped her hands on her apron.

"You're surely right. Fussin' doesn't solve our problem."

"I'm sorry to upset you." Riley moved toward the fire, and his red-brown hair picked up the color of dancing flames.

"I said a few unkind things myself."

"Can you hear me out and ponder over what I say before you give me an answer?" His voice sounded sweeter than a robin's song in spring. She wondered how many other women he'd persuaded in that honeyed tone of voice.

"Yes, I'll do that. Please sit down. Do you want to talk now or after supper?"

Riley moistened his lips. "Probably best to get it all out now. Won't take long." When she nodded, he eased down into the chair. "We don't need to hash over the mistake we made to get out of jail. The deed's done, and neither of us can change it. What we need to decide is how we're going to carry out our married life."

Nettie swallowed hard. Having Riley this close caused emotions to swell that a respectable woman shouldn't think about.

"I don't want to leave Mesquite until I find Abe Wilkins. I'm hoping it won't take more than another day, but I need a place to stay in the meantime. I promise I won't bother you or make you uncomfortable." He pointed in front of the fireplace. "I'd like to sleep here. Folks won't talk, Nettie. After all, we're married."

She stared at the floor, hoping he didn't see what his nearness did to her.

"After I see Mr. Wilkins, I want to make sure you're properly cared for. I'm able to pay a fair price for this land." He held up his hand as though defending himself. "As a man, I want my wife to have a decent home. Once I'm back in Montana, I'll drive a few cattle here to get you started. We'll still be married, but we'll be living in different places." He turned and stared into the fire, then gave her his attention again. "If you meet someone and want to marry him, I won't hold you back."

Why did she suddenly wish Montana wasn't so far away?

seven

Riley ate the scrambled eggs and corn bread in silence. If he'd known what to say, then he'd have offered conversation, but his tongue stayed busy letting his teeth chew. Studying his forkful of food, he believed the eggs reminded him of his brains lately.

Oddly enough, his mind constantly veered to one path—Nettie. She looked powerful pretty with the firelight dancing off her smooth skin and her sparkling gray eyes. She wore a right nice dress of green. His mind lingered on how she'd look with her silky dark hair lying on her shoulders. His reaction to her made no sense at all. It hadn't been but a few hours ago that he'd been ready to escort her to jail, just to be rid of her.

Stabbing his fork into a mound of eggs, he wondered if this was how it felt to be caught in a spider's web. Caught. Trapped. No way out. Except Riley didn't mind a bit, at least not this very moment.

He sat his fork across his tin plate and raised the coffee mug to his lips, all the while pretending interest in supper when he happened to take every opportunity to get a peek at her. Perhaps this feeling stemmed from the fact that Nettie was his wife. After all, husbands and wives did married things.

Riley's own thoughts caused him to feel uneasy. Nettie had a fine reputation as a good woman. At least she did until Judge Balsh had thrown her in jail. She loved the Lord wholeheartedly and wanted to do His will. Riley would not upset her by insisting he had husband rights, when in truth he didn't. The old Riley would have taken advantage of the woman before him, even told her lies and declared empty promises. Not now, not with the Lord directing his life.

Married folks were supposed to love each other and want to stay together for the rest of their lives. And when he considered how the future looked, it seemed best they remain as friends and nothing more.

With a shudder, he realized he best find Abe Wilkins soon.

"I've been thinking," Nettie said, breaking the silence. "I'd like for you to sleep in my bed tonight."

Riley sputtered and choked. He reached for more coffee and burned his tongue in the process. Standing, he headed outside until he regained his senses. Had he been wrong about Nettie all along?

The sky had made its transition from dark blue to nearly black, and stars dotted the heavens. He'd spent many a night sleeping under these twinkling creations. Riley coughed again, and his throat scratched raw.

"Riley?"

He hadn't heard Nettie come up behind him.

"Are you all right? Do you need some water?"

Riley refused to look at her. Even this close scared him, and especially after what she'd said. "I'm fine. Now I know what my ma meant when she said my eating too fast would be the death of me."

Silence made him more than a little nervous with Nettie looking and smelling a whole lot better than his horse.

"What I started to say inside is you've spent many a night outside and in Mesquite's jail. I think it's only proper you should take my bed, and I'll sleep in front of the fire."

Riley groped for his senses. Her words sounded like silk, and the meaning calmed his mind. "That's mighty nice of you, but I'd consider your fireplace a good place to bed down tonight. I don't want to be abusing your hospitality."

She tilted her head. "Oh, you wouldn't. It's the least I could do under the circumstances. If you change your mind, let me know."

"Yes, Ma'am."

"I'm going back inside now. There's plenty of coffee left, and I have a little apple butter for your corn bread."

"I believe I'll check on my horse and your mule before I head back inside."

Nettie turned and walked away. She barely made a noise, but her presence stayed with him like the glow from a field of sunflowers.

I don't have time for any of this nonsense. There're too many other things to keep me busy.

≈

Instead of sleeping that night, Nettie spent most of her time tossing in bed, recalling all the conversations she and Riley had shared in jail and their argument that evening. Most of all, she contemplated why he had such an effect on her. Good looks weren't enough to make a fine husband. Neither did wealth create in her a desire to make the best of this marriage. She desperately craved companionship and possibly a real family in the future. None of which she'd have with Riley. The thought brought unbidden tears to her eyes. She swiped them away and attempted to focus on other things that might bring on sleep.

The following morning, Nettie stepped out of her room to do chores only to see a bucket of milk by the door. She stepped outside to the shadowed morning and waved at him.

"You're spoiling me," she said.

Although she couldn't see his face, she heard his deep chuckle. The sound brought back all the feelings from the night before—the ones she swore to deny. The mere idea of her heart betraying her mind frustrated her. The sooner Riley left, the better.

"I'm heading over to where Abe Wilkins lives," Riley announced at breakfast. "Preacher Faulkner gave me directions."

"Good," Nettie replied, a trifle more cheerful than she felt. "I'm sure you two will have much to talk about."

"Hope so. If all goes well, I'll be leaving this evening or in the morning."

Nettie despised her mixed feelings at the thought of Riley leaving. Soon her life would be back to normal, if such a thing existed. "I plan to till my garden a bit. Weeds are choking my beans."

Riley nodded and left soon afterward. She took her hoe and chopped at those strangling nuisances that threatened the life out of her precious plants. Every weed became a detestable part of her life. She tugged at the bitterness in caring for her ailing parents and leaving behind any hopes of having a family of her own. She didn't regret those years and the tender moments they shared, only the loss. She hadn't contemplated those memories in a long while, but this morning, thinking about Riley and the relationship they'd never have made her weepy. A tear dropped on the wooden handle of the hoe, like a single raindrop, destined to initiate more—which it did.

Maybe she mistook her purpose. Maybe she should have listened harder when God called her to work in the temperance movement. Preacher Faulkner did make a lot of sense about how unbelievers perceived Christians who tossed the fires of wrath into their faces. And he'd made excellent suggestions on how she could reach those for the Lord by simply reaching out in love.

Nettie dried her eyes and straightened her back. The sun beat down hard, causing perspiration mixed with tears to soak her face like healing rain. She took a deep breath and hurriedly finished the chore. She knew what she must do.

Within the hour, she hitched the mule to the wagon and patted the animal as though it were a long-lost friend. Rejoicing in renewed enthusiasm for the Lord's work, she thought the mule might even speak to her like Balaam's donkey. Some wisdom she could use.

Inside the soddie, she washed her face and arms before lacing up her corset so tightly that she could barely breathe, but it did give her the envied hourglass look. She reached for her Sunday dark-brown skirt with a green-and-brown print blouse. Nettie loved the feel of the clothes, although they were faded and worn. Smoothing her hair, she tucked a few stray strands into hairpins, then peeked into the small handheld mirror for the effect. Satisfied, she pulled a trunk from the end of her bed and dug through memorabilia for her savings. Finding the appropriate coins, Nettie closed the trunk and shoved it back into place.

Releasing a satisfied sigh, she headed for the wagon and on into Mesquite. The drive normally took about three-quarters of an hour, but today the time dragged. Nettie sang hymns and talked aloud to God. She felt exhilarated at the thought of God using her in His plan. Once again, she had purpose and meaning in her life.

Nettie pulled the wagon into Mesquite. She wanted to visit with Maudie Mae, but God came first. Afterward, she and her friend could have a lovely chat. Later she'd call on Preacher Faulkner. He'd be so pleased that she had taken his advice.

She tied the reins to a hitching post in front of the general store. Before she headed home, she'd purchase coffee. Riley drank a healthy amount of the dark brew, and her supply had quickly dwindled. She gazed across the street to the saloon. Her pulse quickened and a twinge of fear assaulted her nerves, but her mission would take only a moment, and the result might last for eternity.

Nettie hastened her steps and marched through the swinging doors. Had it been a week ago she had done this same thing? Glancing neither to the right nor to the left, she focused her attention on the barkeeper. He looked up. Lines furrowed his brow. The man opened his mouth to speak, but Nettie held up her hand in defense.

"I only came to apologize," she managed to say through a nervous-sounding breath.

The barkeeper narrowed his gaze.

"I'm sorry for last week. I was terribly wrong to say those things to your customers."

"You're right by that, Lady," the barkeeper said.

A dusty farmer sauntered up to him and asked for a drink. Nettie bit her tongue to keep from quoting Scripture. The notion Preacher Faulkner might be wrong stuck in her mind like taffy that hadn't been buttered. If the preacher's ways didn't secure immediate results, she'd have to risk going to jail again.

Nettie couldn't watch any longer and instead studied a crack in the wooden floor.

"Is there anything else?" the barkeeper asked.

She lifted her head, relieved the dusty farmer no longer stood there. "Yes, I want to pay for Mr. Frank's drink, the one I spilled."

The barkeeper pointed to a table near the door. "He's right over there. Frank," he said, "this here lady would like a word with you."

Frank rose from his chair, the wooden legs scraping across the floor. When he saw Nettie, his face reddened, and he clenched his fists.

"What do you want? I thought the judge took care of you."

Nettie lifted her chin. "He. . .did. I'm here to apologize for what I did to you, and to. . ." She gulped and her knees shook. "Pay you this." She reached in her skirt pocket and with trembling fingers held out the coins sufficient to cover the spilled drink.

"Well, I'll be," Frank said and chuckled. "Maybe I ought to have my wife sit in jail for a few days. Might change her attitude about me."

Nettie bit her tongue to keep from stating what she really thought. "I haven't changed my mind," she said, "but my way didn't honor the Lord."

"Are we back to preaching?" Frank's shout caused her to jump.

A little voice told Nettie to walk out of the saloon and not look back. "No, Sir. I simply stated the truth."

"So you're saying it's all right to drink?" Frank stood close enough for her to smell the rotten liquor on his breath.

"No, Sir." Her voice came in short gasps of air. "I'm saying my way of relaying the information to you was inappropriate, but I would like to invite you to church."

"Nettie, what are you doing in my saloon?" said a familiar booming voice. "You haven't been married two whole days and already you're causing trouble."

"No, Sir, I'm not." Panic crept through Nettie's body, then seized hold of her heart. She turned to face him. "I came here to apologize to the barkeeper and to return Mr. Frank's money."

"Is this true?" The judge whipped his attention to the barkeeper, then to Mr. Frank.

The barkeeper nodded, but Frank held a steady gaze.

"She has me all fired up mad again," Frank said. "I don't 'preciate some woman telling me I need to be in church when I'm having a little drink with my friends."

Nettie caught her breath. "I didn't say you needed to be in church; I invited you."

"Which is it?" Judge Balsh had the loudest voice in town.

"Are you taking her word over mine, a customer?" Frank pounded his fist onto the table. "I've had enough of this church business from them women singing outside the saloon. I thought I'd get a little peace here."

"But Judge," Nettie protested, "that isn't what I said."

Judge Balsh stomped over to Nettie and took her arm. "I'm taking you back to jail."

≈

Riley caught sight of a dugout in the distance. If it hadn't been for the cow and pig tugging at the grass, he'd have missed it for sure. As he rode closer, he made out a small vegetable garden and another dugout used to store hay and animals. The place looked clean and well cared for. From Preacher Faulkner's directions, this had to be Abe Wilkins's place.

"Mr. Abe Wilkins? Are you here?"

From behind the dugout, the old man teetered forward, hunched over and using a walking stick. "What do you want, Son?" Abe asked.

A satisfying feeling soared through Riley. *Thank You, Lord.* "Do you remember me?"

Abe shielded his eyes from the glaring sun. "Don't recollect I do. Could you come a little closer? My eyesight's failing me."

Riley dismounted and in easy strides made it to the old man's side. "Do you remember me now?" He bent so Abe could take a better look.

The old man grinned a toothless smile. "Yes, Sir, I do. I patched you up a few years back after you'd been in a fight."

"That's right. You took care of me when nobody else would. Riley O'Connor's the name."

Abe shook his hand. "I'm glad you made it through all right."

"Well, I'm here to thank you for leading the way."

A curious look passed over Abe's face. "I gave you a Bible, didn't I?"

Riley clasped a hand onto the old man's shoulder. "You did more than give me God's Word. You started me on a journey home."

"You found Jesus." Huge tears rolled down Abe's brown, weathered cheeks.

"Yes, and I turned my life over to Him. So I'm thanking you on two counts."

The old man couldn't say a word, obviously overwhelmed by emotion.

"I bought me a Bible of my own, so I'm returning yours." Riley retrieved the worn Bible from his saddlebag. "Many a night I've studied your notes written beside the Scripture."

Abe turned the Bible over in his hands. "Never thought I'd

see this again. I'm real grateful, but if my notes helped, then I don't want to take them from you."

Riley shook his head. "I copied all of yours into mine."

The old man shed a few more tears. "Won't you set a spell with me? I'd like to hear how your life has changed."

"It might take awhile."

"I have all day. At my age, never know when the good Lord may be calling me home."

eight

Humiliation and despair seeped from the pores of Nettie's skin. Once again Judge Balsh escorted her to jail in the middle of the day for the whole town of Mesquite to see. All of her pleadings for understanding were useless. The judge believed Frank's story rather than hers, although the barkeeper had taken her side.

All because she believed God wanted her to make amends. Hadn't He clearly shown that through Preacher Faulkner's advice?

"Where's Riley?" the judge asked.

"He's out trying to find a man by the name of Abe Wilkins," Nettie replied, holding up her head. She would not succumb to tears. "Riley's a Christian now, and Mr. Wilkins helped him make that decision."

"How ironic. If your husband wants his wife back, he'll have to come up with money to get you out, or he'll join you."

Nettie gasped. "Please, Judge. Don't do this to Riley. He had no part in this."

Judge Balsh drew in his nose as though she hadn't bathed in a month. "Ugh. I don't know which one of you is worse."

Sheriff Kroft did not hesitate to voice his surprise. "Miss Nettie, I thought you'd do anything to keep from coming back to jail. What happened?"

This time, she resolved not to shed a tear in front of the judge or the sheriff. She stiffened. "Is it possible to see Preacher Faulkner?"

The sheriff looked to Judge Balsh for direction. The judge

narrowed his brows. "I guess it won't hurt, but I forbid Maudie Mae to come near this place."

❧

"God is surely moving in your life." A spark of admiration flitted through Abe's clear eyes as he gazed at Riley. "I've always believed He could use those of us who've been down a few crooked roads easier than ones who haven't strayed. We just have more understanding of how deep sin can go."

"You might be right. I've been able to reach a few cowboys who wouldn't step near a church," Riley said. "I'd been in their boots and told them so."

"Sure wish someone could reach my son. He has a good wife and a pretty little daughter, but every day he's drinking up the money that's supposed to go to his family. I was looking for him the night I spied you in the street." Remorse clouded Abe's face.

"I'd be glad to talk to him."

Abe rubbed his whiskered chin. "I wouldn't discourage you, but he's a hard man."

"What's his name?"

"Frank, Frank Wilkins."

Riley thought he'd caught a chicken bone in his throat. This was the man whose drink Nettie had dumped. Why would Frank Wilkins ever listen to Riley? "I'll think on it. I know who you're talking about."

"Thank you. 'Preciate your prayers too." Abe studied him curiously. "Did you say you got married?"

Riley felt a rush of guilt wash over him. "Yeah, and I'm not too proud of it either."

"Why's that?" Abe leaned closer.

"We both were in jail in Mesquite. Nettie was there because the judge charged her with disturbing the peace when she tried to convince folks in his saloon about the evils of drinking. And he didn't like her friendship with his wife either. The judge threw me in there when he thought I'd been drinking when in fact I got hit in the head by a frying pan at the boardinghouse. I'd stopped at the place for a hot meal and walked in on the owners having a disagreement. Then the judge said Nettie must have a family member get her out, so I married her and we were released. Unfortunately, we didn't pray about it."

Abe laughed until tears rolled down his cheeks. He slapped Riley on the back. "I'm sorry, Son, but that's the best story I've heard in a long time."

"Trouble is, it's the truth."

Abe sobered. "Now you have a wife here and a ranch in Montana."

"I'm considering buying the land where she lives from the judge and giving her a few head of cattle. Don't want to worry about her once I'm gone."

"Why isn't she going with you?"

Riley shrugged. "Never thought about it. She was the school-teacher, but after what happened, the school board fired her."

Abe paused and glanced skyward. His lips moved, but he didn't utter a sound. "Ever think God might want you two together?"

"Me and Nettie? Abe, I'm not the marrying type."

"Too late now."

"I—I never looked at it that way." Sweat rolled down past Riley's temples.

"Is she mean spirited? Ugly? Not a believer?"

Riley shook his head. "She's a Christian, right pretty, but a bit high strung."

"Sounds like the makings of a good wife to me. What kind of a real man wants a woman to always agree with him anyway? Makes life interesting." Abe paused. "Son, you're shaking like a leaf. Being a husband got you scared to death?"

Riley wiped his face with his hands. "Reckon so."

"Why don't you go on back and talk to her? Maybe she's scared too."

Riley released a labored breath. Abe hadn't steered him wrong yet, but taking on Nettie as a real wife wasn't what he'd planned—or even thought he wanted.

Abe laid a hand on Riley's shoulder. "Talk to God about it, and I'll be praying the answer will come easy."

Riley's attention focused on the sun beginning its afternoon descent across the sky. He could talk to God on the way back to Nettie's place. "All right, I can do that." He stood up from his chair. "Thank you for talking to me and sharing your noontime food with me."

"And I thank you for returning my Bible and taking the time to let me know what the Lord's doing in your life."

They shook hands, but before Riley realized it, both men were hugging.

While Riley rode toward Nettie's, he pondered Abe's words. The old man had been placed in his path over four years ago for a reason, and he might be again.

"Lord," Riley began aloud as he ambled his chestnut mare along, "I did a foolish thing a few days ago. I know You watched me do it. Right now, I'm not sure what I'm supposed to do with my life or with Nettie. Are You asking me to jump into this husband business? To tell You the truth, I'm right scared. I guess if I think about it, a man must take responsibility for his own actions. Getting married might not have been what You wanted for me, but I've done it." Riley looked at the hills in the distance. "Lord, I sure could use an answer."

His reply didn't come from the heavens or from the mountaintops in the distance. Instead he felt alone and found himself wondering how Nettie spent her day.

Once back at the soddie, he looked inside and out for her. Wherever Nettie had gone, she'd taken the mule and wagon. Seeing the sun dip down toward evening, he figured she'd be back soon. In the meantime, he'd milk the cow and tend to a few things around the place.

Within thirty minutes, he heard a rider call his name. "Riley, are you here?"

He stepped from the dugout and viewed Preacher Faulkner glancing about a bit anxiously. "Something wrong?"

Preacher Faulkner pushed his black hat back from his head and leaned on his saddle horn. "I'd say so."

A sinking feeling about Nettie sent a prickle at his nape. "Is this about my wife?"

" 'Fraid so. She up and got herself arrested again. Judge Balsh threw her in jail."

Riley clenched his jaw. "Didn't she learn the first time?"

Preacher Faulkner dismounted from his horse. "Don't get riled. I think the whole thing is a misunderstanding. See, I suggested she do good works for those she wanted to dissuade from alcohol instead of condemning them. Well, she went into the saloon and apologized to the barkeeper, then returned Frank Wilkins's money. Frank took the money, then told the judge she was preaching at him again. She told me she had only invited him to church, and her invite made him mad."

Riley moaned. Naturally the judge would take a customer's word over Nettie's. He wouldn't be surprised if she had been preaching. Why did Frank have to be Abe's son?

"Let me saddle up my horse. She's my responsibility, you know."

"I know," Preacher Faulkner said. "I believe she's innocent, but the judge refused to let her out."

All the way into town with the preacher, Riley fought the anger swelling inside him. Couldn't Nettie just stay home and leave well enough alone? He wanted to talk to her tonight, not sweet-talk the judge into letting her go. How could Riley get things straightened out about their marriage when she'd run off to town?

"Why couldn't she leave that temperance stuff alone?" he asked.

"Because Nettie is the type of woman who fights for what she believes," Preacher Faulkner replied. "And that characteristic isn't bad, although she might need to change her manner of going about it."

"Amen." Riley wished he knew what to say to her about this second arrest. He didn't want to quarrel with her, but provoked, he could hold his own in any argument. God said a man should be the head of his household and to love his wife as Christ loves the church. In turn the woman was to be submissive. Something told him Nettie would battle him for the rest of his life about submission.

Riley and Preacher Faulkner tied their horses to the hitching post outside the jail. Riley couldn't decide if he wanted to fetch Nettie or leave her alone. The thought of riding on to Montana did cross his mind.

"Riley, Preacher Faulkner," Sheriff Kroft said in greeting, much too friendly to Riley's way of thinking. The sheriff sat with his feet propped on the roughly constructed desk with his head cradled in his hands. Didn't the man ever do anything worthwhile? "I figured you'd be here shortly after nightfall."

Nettie stood up from the cot inside the cell—the same cell she'd occupied before. Riley curbed his tongue by refusing to meet her gaze. At this very minute, he'd like to turn her across his knee.

"How do I get my wife released?" Riley asked. "I'm sure Judge Balsh mentioned I'd be asking."

"He shore did," the sheriff said. "Said it would cost twenty-five dollars."

"Twenty-five dollars!" Riley felt the heat rise in his face. "What did she do, rob a bank?"

Sheriff Kroft grinned, revealing a few missing teeth. "The

judge said you wouldn't like the price, but you can always join her, being newlyweds and all."

Riley had yet to look at Nettie. Fury at her and the judge had taken away all his joy from visiting Abe.

"I don't have but six dollars at home," Nettie said.

Her weak-sounding voice caught his attention, and he whirled around to make sure she hadn't been abused.

"Are you all right?" Riley scuffed his boot against the floor. He'd rather stomp his foot through the floor.

"Yes, I'm fine," she said in a timid reply. "Riley, all I have to my name is six dollars."

"I heard you the first time, but I don't have but ten left over from purchasing supplies." He started to give her a good tongue-lashing, but at the sight of those huge gray eyes, he couldn't quite remember why he'd been angry.

"I'll see what I can do." A sense of protectiveness swept over him. "Don't worry, I'll get you out of here."

She nodded and lifted her chin, just as he'd seen her do when they'd been in jail together. He whirled around to face Preacher Faulkner and Sheriff Kroft. "I'll be back in a little bit with the money. Thank you, Preacher Faulkner, for fetching me and explaining what happened."

"You're welcome." The preacher glanced about the jail. "I think I'll sit here for awhile to keep Nettie company."

Sheriff Kroft moaned, but the preacher ignored him. Rather than comment, Riley left his wife in the company of the two men. He headed toward the livery. The owner there had offered to buy his saddle, but Riley hadn't been interested at the time. Parting with his saddle made him a little more frustrated than he'd been earlier. The way Riley looked at the circumstances, he didn't have much choice. The Bible said to give it all away in love. The giving he could do.

Within the hour, he walked back into the sheriff's office and handed him the twenty-five dollars. The saddle had been worth nearly twice that, but he didn't have time to haggle over the price. Without a word, Sheriff Kroft unlocked Nettie's cell, and she stepped out. For the first time, he noticed she wore a nice dress.

"I appreciate this," Nettie said, but he refused to acknowledge her or her words.

Riley tipped his hat to the preacher and opened the door for his wife. He suddenly questioned the logic of a wife being a helpmate. She more closely resembled a bad hangover.

All the way home, Nettie said nothing. She sat with her hands in her lap while Riley drove the wagon. He'd tied his saddleless horse to the rear wagon. How long must he go without another one? Wiring the town nearest his ranch for more money made the best sense.

At Nettie's place, she followed him into the dugout. He grabbed an oil lantern from the back of the wagon and lit it.

"It's been a long day and an even longer evening," Riley said. "Why don't you go on to bed? I'll handle the wagon and animals."

"It's important to me that you know the truth." She wrung her hands as though she intended to wash them.

"Preacher Faulkner told me."

"And you believe me?" Her words reminded Riley of a little girl, not the feisty woman who dared to stand for the temperance movement.

Did he really believe her? "Yes, I do, Nettie, but I don't understand why you went there in the first place."

"To be like Jesus—to bring food to the women working there, and more importantly to apologize to the barkeeper and to give Mr. Frank his money back."

How could Riley fault her for following the preacher's suggestions?

When he didn't respond, she continued. "Frank lied to the judge."

"I know," he said. Suddenly her sweet voice had gotten to him.

"I never. . ." She muffled a sob. "I never wanted you to sell your fine saddle. It will take a long time for me to save enough money to buy another one. Maudie Mae couldn't help me because the judge wouldn't let her near the jail."

The weeping pressed against his heart. "Don't fret about it, Nettie. I have means of getting a new saddle."

"But it's my responsibility, my fault. I'll be thanking you for the rest of my life for all you've done for me." She tilted her head. "Did you find Abe Wilkins?"

The change of topic helped relax Riley. "Yes, I did. We spent a good bit of the day talking." Then he remembered what Abe suggested about Nettie and praying about their marriage. Frank Wilkins was Abe's son, but Riley didn't feel like telling her that bit of news. Most likely she'd find out soon enough.

"I'm glad for you." She stood by while he unhitched the mule.

"Without a saddle, I'm gonna need to stay around awhile."

Silence.

"I wish you'd say something." The familiar frustration inched through him.

"Well, we are married, and you do need a place to live."

All the fight seemed to be gone from her, and he almost missed it. "I'd like for us to work toward a better relationship."

"In what way?"

Riley felt the back of his neck grow wet. Never had a woman affected him like this. "Friends first, then I thought we could look into the possibility of God wanting us to have a real married life."

For the first time, he saw Nettie appear not to know what to say.

"I mean He put us together for a reason," Riley continued, "and I hope it's not to kill each other fighting." He meant for his latter remark to be funny, but she didn't even smile.

When he looked into her face with the lantern light dancing off her hair, he caught his breath. A man could do a whole lot worse than Nettie Franklin O'Connor. Right then, Riley couldn't think of a more beautiful woman in all of Nebraska.

"Quarreling makes me furious at myself," she said. "I don't have a terrible temper. It's simply the words come flying out of my mouth before I can stop them."

"I used to have a bad way about settling disputes, but that's not God honoring. What do you say? Can we give this marriage a try?"

"I'd like to." Nettie turned away. "I—I need to milk the cow."

"I already did before riding into town."

"Thank you." She bordered on tears. "Preacher Faulkner came by every day when I was in jail and milked for me. His wife brought me fresh-baked bread. But they. . ." Nettie nearly broke down. "But they did those things because God called them to show His love for others. You do good things because you're a good man."

"Don't make me out to be more than I am." Riley led the mule to its stall. "I've done more than my share of sinnin'. Remember me in Archerville?" Right now, he'd shovel out manure from here to Montana to keep from looking at Nettie and listening to how good she thought he was.

"Those things are true, except you have courage, Riley. You had courage to change and give God all the credit."

He shook his head and wished she would stop goin' on. *Please, Lord, this is downright humiliating.*

"Have you eaten?" she asked.

"At midday." Should he ask her to fix a skillet of corn bread? At least then she'd be in the house and out of sight.

"You must be starved. I'll see what I can rustle up. I'll put on a pot of coffee first."

"I am powerful hungry. Did anyone bring you supper tonight?"

"Sheriff Kroft brought a plate from the boardinghouse."

"Then you're hungry too." He gave her a smile and watched her disappear.

Riley let out a sigh and shivered in the warm night. Why did pleasing Nettie and letting her know she was special suddenly mean more to him than anything else going on in his life?

nine

Nettie trembled as she tossed a few cow chips into the fireplace, then struck a match against a rock to light it. Within minutes she had a good fire started for supper. She measured coffee beans for the grinder and snatched up the coffeepot. Her mind spun with all the events of the day and how she'd once more ended up in jail for doing God's work. Either God hadn't called her into the temperance movement, or she was going about His business the wrong way, because every move shoved her deeper into trouble.

What really upset her came in a word: Riley. He'd repeatedly sacrificed his time and money to help her. First he'd been duped into marrying her and then this evening he'd been forced to sell his saddle. Her six dollars looked like a poor start to repay Riley, and without a job, she worried when she'd have the rest of the money.

What could she do? In most places married women didn't teach school, and besides she had no plans of moving from Mesquite. The thought of heading back to Archerville crossed her mind. No, she'd be too embarrassed if folks asked about what happened in Mesquite. Where could she live once the school board found a new teacher? Riley had graciously offered to purchase the place from the judge, but Nettie dare not accept any more of his generosity.

Mesquite had a fine midwife. Nettie could visit with her and see if she needed any help. The woman had a sweet disposition, and they'd spent time talking about bringing children into the world. Nettie hated losing her teaching position. She'd loved children for as long as she could remember. God must have something better in mind, and she must continue to believe those words.

Nettie dropped a few of the precious coffee beans and snatched them up from the floor. Grinding them sufficiently, she added water to the coffeepot. What really had her mind in a tizzy centered on her reaction to Riley in the barn. She'd behaved like a girl instead of a mature woman. And for the life of her, she couldn't figure out why. For now she'd toss the matter aside. Too many other problems plagued her mind without adding another.

All the while she stirred together the corn bread, she attempted to focus on what God wanted for her life. Without a doubt, the temperance movement met the most resistance, so she must be doing the right thing. The problem must be in her approach. Neither her method nor Preacher Faulkner's had caused a single one of those using strong drink to change from their sinful ways.

The door creaked open, and Riley stepped in. She shuddered and ordered herself not to look at him for any length of time before her heart betrayed her guarded emotions.

"The coffee will be done in a few minutes." She bustled about the small soddie. "Corn bread too."

"Thank you." Riley sat in one of the two chairs. Instantly he stood and the chair went crashing to the dirt floor.

"What's wrong?" No sooner had the words left her lips than she saw a rattler coiled near the fire where she'd placed the skillet of corn bread. She gasped.

"Open the door," he said. In an instant he grabbed up her broom and lifted the snake, hissing and spitting, to the outside.

Nettie lifted the rifle from above the door and handed it to him. In the next breath, a shot fired, making a short end to the rattler. For the third time this evening, her emotions got the best of her and she shook from head to toe. What if

Riley had been bitten? God must be punishing her for something horrible she'd done.

"Coffee done?" Riley shut the door behind him and righted the chair.

"You didn't get hurt?" Fear washed over her for this dear man who had rescued her time and time again.

"No, Ma'am, but Nettie, you need to take heed around here. Snakes love to wiggle through the roof. That one could have bitten you while you were about the fire. And what if I hadn't been here? Why, you'd be dead." He took off his hat and laid it on the table. "Promise me you'll take care of yourself."

"I'll do better." It wasn't the first time a rattler had fallen through the roof, but she didn't feel inclined to expound on that information. Snakes and bugs were a fact of life in a soddie. He should know those things.

"I built my house in Montana out of wood. There's not a shortage of trees there." He raked his fingers through his hair.

She ignored his obvious discomfort and poured him a cup of coffee. "Tell me about your ranch. Do you run many cattle?"

A slow grin spread over his face. How interesting. She'd just used a technique she'd learned during her teaching days to handle an upset child: change the subject. Looked like it worked on a man too.

"I have about a thousand head of cows, and new calves come spring." He paused, and his easy smile lingered. "God's been good to me, Nettie. When I came to Montana, I hired on for a man who didn't have much money to pay me, but he gave me a place to live and food to eat. I worked hard—like the Bible says—work as though you're working for God. He started giving me a cow or a calf when the ranch made money. He paid me when he could, and I saved it. In about two years, I had a small herd. We made a deal, and he sold me several hundred acres and more cattle to start my own place. I built a house and barn but kept helping him too. I hired a trustworthy man, Sam Rafford, as foreman when I left, but I do need to get back."

"Is it green and pretty?" Nettie bent to pull the skillet off the fire. Once she set the corn bread on the table, she put a generous hunk on a plate for Riley and rested a fork beside it. A jug of sorghum and a small amount of butter would top their supper nicely.

He nodded and picked up the fork. "In the spring and summer, the land is green enough to hurt your eyes. The grass is thick, and the cows grow fat. In the distance you have mountains, more than here. The streams are clear, and the air breathes fresh, giving a man strength to do whatever God sets before him."

"I think you've found your heaven, Riley."

"Maybe so." His attention settled on her, and he smiled even broader. "I bet you'd like Montana, Nettie, although the womenfolk aren't as many as here. Folks live far apart and few between. Doesn't matter to me. I like the open spaces."

"Sounds nice, but I need to be around people. Don't know what I'd do without Maudie Mae."

"Most menfolk think differently," he said.

When she failed to think of a proper response, she took up a plate and cut a piece of corn bread for herself. He kept taking quick glances at her, for what reason Nettie had no idea. Finally he scooted back at his place.

"You sure can make tasty corn bread," he said. "Thank you. I know it's late, and you've had a hard day."

She poured both of them another cup of coffee. "I enjoy cooking."

Silence beset them—and she'd always prided herself on taking up the slack in conversation. Riley rested his elbows on the table.

"Is there something you want to say?" Nettie asked after several long moments. "If it's the money—"

He shook his head. "No, I'm not concerned about the money. You don't owe me a thing. It's. . .it's something else."

She peered into his rugged face and those blue eyes that seemed to melt her like sunshine melted snow on a spring day.

"I've been thinking." He leaned back in the chair and stole a look at the fire. "Nettie, have you ever been courted?"

Color warmed her face, and she guessed he had his answer.

"I'm still wondering if this marriage thing would work for us."

Dumbfounded, Nettie said nothing.

"I'd like to ease into it, if you were agreeable. I like talking with you, and we are married. But. . .have you been thinking on it?"

Rather than lie, Nettie dampened her dry lips. "I'm surprised at what you're asking. Truthfully, I never thought I'd be a wife. I'm a little beyond the marrying age."

"Nettie, you're downright pretty. And I'm surprised you've never been asked."

Before she knew it, Nettie was in the middle of telling Riley about tending to her ill parents. "I'm glad I nursed Mama and Papa, and I never regretted it at the time." She shrugged. "My commitment to them meant I passed up any marriage proposals."

"You're married now," he said.

The tenderness in Riley's voice caused a fluttering in her stomach.

"I'm not asking for things about a man and wife that's private. In my mind, those times ought to wait. I spent too many years of my life taking advantage of women." He gulped. "I believe a husband and a wife should have feelings for each other first."

Nettie knew her face flamed hotter than the fire. "I understand what you're saying."

"Are you willing to try?"

Nettie's heart and stomach were all churned together. More

than anything, she wanted to have Riley court her. Oh, but it scared her worse than any rattler. What about her temperance movement and the things Preacher Faulkner suggested? What if her and Riley's relationship really was a blessing? What if someday they might have a family of their own? Nettie swallowed hard. What if Riley wanted to move to Montana? She couldn't ever leave Maudie Mae and not be around people. Worse yet, what if Riley felt obligated to her? Then Nettie remembered her vows. She'd always believed a Christian should keep a promise to God. After all, He kept His promises.

Nettie sinned enough without realizing it; committing one on purpose sounded terribly wicked to her. If God willed her and Riley to find love, then she'd do her part.

"I believe I want to try," Nettie said barely above a whisper.

Riley took her hand. "Then let's ask the good Lord to bless our marriage."

She bowed her head, eager to hear how Riley spoke to the Lord. She felt blessed and special at the same time.

"Heavenly Father, me and Nettie come to You tonight with a heavy burden on our hearts. We're married and we don't know what to do about it. I mean, You witnessed it all. Right now, we're asking You to show us the way. Neither of us ever thought we'd be married, but we are. Lord, we want to try to work something out here—to find a reason to stay together married-like. We need help and we're asking for it. In Your Son's name, amen."

Riley lifted his head. "Did I sound all right to you?"

Nettie fought to keep her tears away from his sight. "You prayed just fine, Riley, and I'm real honored you sought the Lord in this bee's nest we're in."

He patted her hand. "Starting right now, I'm gonna try extra hard to be a good husband for you, Nettie. With the Lord's help, we could turn this bee's nest into a home full of honey."

Nettie couldn't stop the tears. Never had a man spoken

such sweet words to her, and never had she been so happy in her life.

"Now, Nettie, why are you crying?"

She swiped at her tears with her free hand. "I'm just scared and happy at the same time. I'm going to do my best too. The future makes me a bit skittish, but if God is on our side, it will turn out just fine."

"I reckon some parts won't be easy."

"I reckon not."

ten

The days moved into weeks, and before Nettie realized it, four weeks had gone by since she and Riley had started working on being friends. His foreman in Montana wired him money for a new saddle, which suited Riley just fine. School started, and for the first time in three years, she had no reason to dust off her McGuffy reader and tidy up the schoolhouse.

Riley had helped her in the garden two weeks ago, and together they'd dried the rest of the green beans, corn, squash, and pumpkins. The cold weather would not find Nettie hungry and depending on the folks from church to supply her with food. Riley made arrangements with a neighbor to purchase corn for the livestock during the winter months, and he did repairs on the soddie and dugout.

"Would you like to gather walnuts today?" Riley asked one morning at breakfast. He dipped his spoon into a bowl of cornmeal mush sweetened with sorghum molasses. "I'm caught up on repairs, and we could make a day of it."

"That sounds like a wonderful idea. I have turkey from last night, one tomato left, corn bread, and some elderberry cobbler," Nettie said.

"We could probably pick some more elderberries on the way back. I do believe those are my favorite," Riley said, patting his stomach.

Every time Nettie looked at him, she loved him more than the day before. At times she stopped herself before touching his face or offering to massage his muscled shoulders bulging beneath his shirt. Riley impressed her with his gentle words and the way he looked out for her. Impossible as it sounded, the other problems in her life didn't matter anymore. A few times she fretted about not having a job or having missed a temperance meeting, but for the first time in her life, she'd allowed a man inside her heart.

A letter went out to her dear friends, Gabe and Lena Hunters, about her marriage to Riley. She knew they would want to hear how God had changed him. Never in all of her born days would Nettie have guessed she'd be Mrs. Riley O'Connor. In fact, she never thought she'd be Mrs. Anybody.

In short order, Riley hitched up the wagon and added a couple of wooden buckets, two feed sacks, and Nettie's makings for their noon meal. Soon they headed across the valley to a wooded area loaded with walnut trees. The air still held all the warm temperatures of summer, but in another month, fall would usher in cooler weather. The day put her in a lighthearted mood, or maybe her bliss could be attributed to Riley's companionship.

"Watch out for snakes," Riley called as he dropped handful after handful of walnuts into his bucket.

"Yes, Sir, I am." How good it felt to have him concerned about her welfare. She'd killed a bushel basket full of snakes in her day, but he didn't need to know that. "Won't be long before these leaves change color."

"Reckon so. Makes me feel like a kid again, listening to them rustle and wanting to jump into a whole pile of them. You should see the Montana mountains in the fall—gold, red, and orange, as though they're competing with summer."

"Why, Riley O'Connor, are you a poet?" She giggled at the confused look on his face.

"Don't think so." He shuffled his boot across the earthen floor, much like she'd seen her students do at school. Glancing up at her laughing, he frowned. "Are you making fun of me?"

"Sure looks like it."

"Nobody laughs at Riley O'Connor unless they want a good thrashing."

He started toward her, but she lifted her skirts above her ankles and ran. Nettie's sides ached from laughing.

"I'll catch you before you get far," Riley said. She heard his deep belly chuckle and hurried faster.

In the next moment, his arms grabbed her waist and they both fell. Riley cradled her just as they hit the ground, as though she were but a little girl and he the protector. Looking up into his eyes—the same color as the ceiling of blue above them—Nettie felt her heart pound hard against her chest.

He rolled onto the colorful blanket, then propped himself up with his elbow to peer anxiously at her. A drop of perspiration trickled down Riley's face. His laughing stopped and his breath came in short, quick gasps. "Are you hurt?"

Nettie smiled. "No, I had my warrior watching over me."

He stroked her hair back from her face. "You have the most beautiful hair, so soft and shiny."

She could only imagine how unkempt it looked with the tumble.

"You're prettier than all the wildflowers put together," he said.

She shivered. "I've never had anyone say such nice things to me."

"Any single man who didn't look your way and appreciate your lovely face must have been blind."

Nettie touched the scar running down his face. For days she'd wanted to do this.

"Does it bother you?" he asked.

"Not at all. It shows your struggle between good and evil. I love it." There she'd said it, the four-letter word that ushered in fear and joy at the same time.

Riley leaned closer. Nettie realized he wanted to kiss her, and she wanted him to—badly. His mouth lowered to hers, and he gently eased his lips overtop hers. She met his kiss with the emotions she'd concealed for the past weeks. Her hand slipped from his face to behind his neck, drawing him closer and allowing him to deepen the moment. His lips tasted warm and sweet.

When the kiss ended, Riley planted another one on the tip of her nose. "I think we need to get back to picking up walnuts," he said, "or I might have to claim another one of those."

"And I might not be able to stop you," she said, surprised at her own boldness.

Riley's gaze heated her heart. She saw the look a man was supposed to give only his wife. They'd passed a milestone with one kiss, and Nettie didn't regret it at all.

❧

Riley found it difficult to concentrate on gathering walnuts. He could barely taste the hearty lunch Nettie had prepared. He tried to listen to her chatter and offer logical comments, but his mouth went dry and his heart pounded faster than the twitch of a rabbit's nose. Later on, when they stopped to pick elderberries, the same notion continued to attack him.

He'd fallen in love with Nettie, and the thought sent tremors up and down his spine. Was this what God intended? How could he keep a wife here in Nebraska and have a ranch in Montana? The last few weeks had been as close to heaven as he figured a man could get on earth. Just looking at Nettie, being around her, made him wonder if he could ever leave Mesquite again. Riley had touched on the tender nature of a godly woman. He stared at the purple stains on his hands. Like those elderberries, she had gotten into his skin and left an impression on his heart.

❧

The sun had descended almost to the horizon when Riley and Nettie returned to the small soddie. He helped her from the wagon and started to unhitch the wagon from the mule.

"Riley?"

He tried not to look into her face, but the sound of her voice reminded him of angels. "Yes."

"Are you angry with me?"

The idea confused him. "Why would you ask such a thing?"

She shrugged. "I mean you kissed me. . .well, I kissed you back, and you haven't been the same since. I thought maybe I didn't do it right."

Her response startled him. "Nettie, you did just fine."

"All right. Are you regretting it?"

Did she have to ask the same questions he wrestled with? "I don't think so. Are you? I probably should have asked first."

"I didn't mind at all." She wrung her hands in front of her. "Do you want to talk about it?"

Riley pushed his hat back and rested his hands on the side of the wagon. "Not yet. I have to think on it awhile first."

Was he seeing things or did tears well up in her gray eyes?

"I'll be inside, fixing us something to eat," she whispered.

"Good, Nettie. That sounds real good. We've had a long day. Don't make a fuss."

She nodded and walked toward the soddie. Her slender figure and the sway of her body caused his mouth to go dry again. It took all Riley's might to stop from going after her and tasting those sweet lips again.

I'm in trouble, here. Big trouble.

❧

The following morning, Riley decided to pay Abe a visit. He needed a long ride to think about Nettie, and a good talk with the Lord would put his life in a better perspective. Visiting with Abe to discuss his dilemma sounded good too. Every time he talked to the old man, God used Abe to steer Riley in the right direction.

Nettie didn't have much to say last night or this morning. Riley knew he should be the one to make conversation about the kiss, but the words refused to form in his mouth.

"I'll be back later," Riley said after breakfast. "I want to check on Abe. An old man needs folks to look after him."

"I agree." Nettie avoided his gaze. "He's welcome here anytime. Please let him know I always have food and shelter for him."

Her concern for Abe pierced his heart. "I will," Riley said. "I appreciate your willingness to take care of him."

"Offering the soddie is the least I can do for the man who helped lead you to the Lord."

Riley tried to respond but couldn't think of a single intelligent thing.

All the way to Abe's place, his mind wavered between the longing he felt for Montana and his increasing emotions for Nettie. She'd never leave Mesquite; she'd said so some weeks before. *Why must this be so hard, Lord? Isn't a woman supposed to follow her husband?*

But they weren't married in the traditional way. Riley pondered and prayed until he saw Abe's soddie. The sight of the old man eased Riley's spirit, and he felt certain the right answers were within eyesight.

"Good to see you, Son," Abe called. Seemed like the man looked paler than the last visit, and he moved slower. "You must have decided to see what God had in mind for you and your bride."

Riley couldn't help but grin, despite his problems with Nettie. "You're right there. I should have stopped by here sooner—"

"You've been spending time with your wife. That's more important. I'm fine, doing fine."

Riley scrutinized Abe. Unless a miracle occurred, the old man would soon be in the arms of Jesus. He remembered Frank. "Has your son been by?"

Abe shook his head. "No, but his kind wife and daughter come regular." He motioned to Riley. "Come sit a spell. I'll get us a glass of cool water, and you can tell me all about what's going on with you."

For the next two hours, Riley poured out his guts about

Nettie, Montana, and the Lord. Then he'd remember something else and talk a little more.

"Hmm," Abe said. "You do have a bit of trouble here. I will say your first commitment, after the Lord, is Nettie. You don't know for sure, she might just jump at the chance of moving to Montana."

"Can't say." Riley kicked at the dirt beneath his feet. "I suppose I could ask."

"Do you love her?" Abe's gaze seemed to peer straight through him.

Riley knew the answer. "I believe I do."

"Let God and your feelings for Nettie guide you. Love can be rather peculiar. To some folks it makes 'em selfish. To others, the one they love can do no wrong. Love means you want the best for the other person, even if the best ends up hurting you."

Riley didn't understand all of what Abe had to say, but he grasped most of it. A Christian man didn't want to be selfish and mean, like he'd seen some husbands be in the past. By demanding Nettie join him in Montana, he might lose her. If he allowed Nettie to make all of the decisions, then Riley wouldn't be completing the role of a real husband. Loving a woman wasn't easy. What did folks do without the Lord?

He said his good-byes to Abe and left a short while later, prepared to talk to Nettie about Montana and his newfound feelings for her.

Midway back to the soddie, Riley spotted a cluster of goldenrods nodding their heads in the August breeze. He stopped his mare and picked several. Nettie liked flowers, and he probably needed a little extra going for his side.

The moment he rode in, she hurried from the house. Worried lines etched across her forehead.

"Are you ailing, Nettie?" Riley asked, dismounting his horse.

She shook her head, and he saw her eyes puddle with water.

"Something happen to upset you?"

Again she shook her head.

"Then what's wrong? You aren't normally like this."

Nettie buried her face in her hands. "Oh, Riley, I was afraid you weren't coming back."

He couldn't handle the tears, not from this precious lady. Riley extended his fist full of goldenrods. "Of course, I planned to come back. I visited a long spell with Abe and stopped to bring you these."

She lifted her head and cried at the sight of the wildflowers. "These are beautiful. I feel so foolish."

Riley took a step forward and gathered her up in his arms. She smelled like flowers, only better. "You can stop those crazy notions right now. We're having a little difficult time with being newly married, but I'd never just ride off and not come back."

Nettie nodded and wiped away her tears. "I'll go put these in some water."

"Not yet." The words were spoken before he had a chance to stop them. When she glanced up, his legs felt like thick sorghum. His lips found hers, and his hand slipped around her trim waist and drew her close.

This time when the kiss ended, neither of them pulled away. Nettie rested her head against his chest, and he buried his face in her hair.

"I've always wondered how all that black hair would look down," he said, his voice a bit husky.

Nettie reached up and pulled out one pin, then another. "A man should see his wife's hair about her shoulders."

He grasped her fingers and kissed them. "I love you, Nettie O'Connor."

"And I love you."

He lifted her into his arms and kissed her again. Soft black hair fell over the back of his hand. "I want to be a good husband," he said.

She smiled adoringly into his face. "Now is a *good* time."

eleven

Nettie wrapped her shawl tighter around her shoulders. The chickens needed to be fed, and she'd brought a basket to gather eggs. Her small flock had increased and provided more eggs than she could use. The little extra money earned by selling them to folks in Mesquite had established a bit of savings.

The judge hadn't decided about selling the land yet, and Riley had agreed to pay rent each month. The town had found a new schoolteacher, but she was the daughter of one of the farmers and didn't need Nettie and Riley's soddie. At first the prospect of another person teaching her dear children depressed Nettie, but the school board didn't want a woman who'd been in jail or gotten married. The business of not teaching school had worked out for the best, even if Nettie sorely missed the children. God had blessed her with the love of a good man, something she'd thought she would never find.

If someone had told her that a godly husband would make a wonderful difference in her life, she'd have hotly denied the need. But Riley's love embraced her with happiness and a sense of fulfillment unlike she'd ever imagined. All of the secret dreams she had abandoned as a girl now showered her many times over. Every day with her husband brought joy and an adventure. The love they shared had come from God, and with His guidance, they'd honor Him all of their lives.

A gust of wind whipped across her face, and she caught her breath. The late summer had been a little chilly, and the thought of an early winter didn't rest well. Dipping temperatures and blizzards always brought an onslaught of fear, but not this year. God had given her Riley, and her husband had made life so much easier. When the winter winds blew, they would have plenty of dried fruits, vegetables, and meat. Cow chips were stacked beside the soddie along with a supply of firewood that Riley had gathered on one of his trips to see Abe.

Nettie loved Abe Wilkins. The old man possessed more wisdom in his little finger than most folks accumulated over their entire lives. His way of looking at life never deviated from the Bible. He had a way of taking the Scriptures and applying them to a situation, then pointing out how God's Word ministered to folks today. A few times Abe had spent the night with her and Riley. He always thanked her for the hospitality, but he longed to be at his own home. Nettie and Riley fretted over his health. Abe looked more frail each time they saw him.

"What better place to meet Jesus than my own home?" Abe said. "I'm looking forward to it, except I'd like to see my son come to the Lord first."

"Does he live near here?" Nettie asked. They were enjoying a cup of coffee around Abe's fireplace. She'd brought lunch and the visit had lasted until late afternoon.

"I haven't told her," Riley said to Abe. "Guess I should have, but I wanted to spare her the heartache."

Nettie glanced from Abe to Riley. "I don't understand. Who is he?"

Abe cleared his throat. "The town drunk, Frank Wilkins."

She felt the color leave her face, and she peered at Riley. "You mean the same Frank whose drink I spilled and who made sure I went to jail—twice?"

Riley nodded.

Nettie caught Abe's gaze, and she slid from the chair to the floor beside him. "I'm so sorry, Abe. I didn't know. I've been praying for him, but I'll do even more."

"Alcohol has become his god." Abe's lips pressed tightly together. "And that demon whiskey is about to destroy his marriage, everything in his life."

Nettie immediately felt regret for abandoning her temperance activities. She should contact Frank's wife. "Is his wife a believer?"

"Says she is, but she doesn't attend church regular. I used to think she was embarrassed with the way Frank carried on, but now I think she's bitter, and that saddens me."

Nettie picked up his veined hand and stroked it lightly. "I understand all too well." For a moment she considered telling him about her parents but changed her mind. Riley didn't know the whole story yet.

"I've tried talking to Frank," Riley said. Nettie felt his hand on her shoulder. "He got powerful mad when I invited him and his family for supper. Said he didn't have time to make conversation with a temperance woman and an old drunk."

Nettie cringed as she remembered how Riley had felt so defeated. She'd held him close and reminded him that God looks at a man's heart, not at the things he'd done in the past. And to think the man was Abe's son.

"Well, I appreciate what you did. Last I heard, his wife was taking in washin' to buy food." Abe's eyes watered.

"What's her name?" Nettie asked.

"Celia, and my granddaughter is Mary."

Nettie managed a smile for the dear old man. "I'll pay them a visit and take a meal. Don't worry, I won't preach or anything like I used to do. I'll simply be Jesus to them."

Riley squeezed her shoulders lightly. She felt his love all the way to her toes.

"Thank you, Nettie," Abe said. "Enough of this gloom. I'd like to have another piece of that apple pie and hear some more tales about the days when you taught school."

On the ride back, Nettie considered the problems plaguing poor Abe. How could Frank treat him so shamefully? She rocked gently with the swaying motion of the wagon, her mind dwelling on the greatness of God. She knew from experience that a person who drank heavily always caused their family heartache. Abe deserved better. Frank deserved better.

The following morning, Nettie searched for Riley with a fresh cup of hot coffee in her hand. His whistling directed her to behind the dugout, where he gazed out over the plain.

"You sound happy this morning," she said, reaching around his waist to give him a hug.

"I am," he said. "I'm thinking about something too."

"Which is?"

"My ranch in Montana."

Nettie felt her emotions plummet. Since the judge had agreed they could live on the land and pay rent, she'd chosen to push Riley's ranch from her mind.

"Don't look so sad," Riley said.

She forced a smile. "What are you wanting to do about it?"

"I've been thinking it all over, and I really want us living there. Even Abe agrees with me."

Immediately betrayal raced through her heart. "You talked to Abe before me?"

"Now, Honey, only for advice." He walked toward her, his blue eyes fixed on her. "I've thought and thought about this. Leaving Abe behind bothers me some, especially with things not settled about his son, but I miss my land. Once we get moved, you'll love it there."

His words became a whirlwind of confusion. Nettie thought Riley had given up on leaving Mesquite. She'd told him about never wanting to leave Maudie Mae and her church family. "No, Riley. I don't want to live anywhere but here."

He frowned. "My home is in Montana where my ranch is. I've been gone much too long. My responsibility is—"

"To me. Your wife." She trembled and attempted to dispel her anger and disappointment.

"It is." Riley's soft tone irritated her even more. "Our future is in Montana. Don't you think if I saw the same possibilities here, I'd be driving my herd in this direction?"

"But what about me? You know how I feel."

Riley took in a deep breath and walked around to the front of the dugout.

"Where are you going?" A twinge of regret washed over her. She should have been calmer, sweeter.

He stopped and, without facing her, he said, "A wife's place is with her husband."

"A husband needs to understand his wife's feelings."

This time, he ambled back to her. "Nettie, I love you. You know that. Look around you." He waved his hand. "I'm not a farmer, never will be, never want to be. I'm a cattleman, and my ranch is the best place to run them cows. All I'm asking is for you to join me before the weather gets bad. I believe once you're there, you'll never look back."

She shook her head. Anger replaced any reason. "I can't do that. My home is here. You don't understand me at all."

"What is so all fired up important about Mesquite? You came here from Archerville, didn't you?"

"I came so I could teach school. You have no idea how hard it was for me, leaving everything behind."

Riley rubbed his scar. "Guess I don't. Where would this country be if all the wives refused to travel into new parts?"

"Maybe you should have gotten yourself a wife who had an adventurous spirit."

"I didn't have a choice." Riley's words were cold, unfeeling. He'd chipped a piece of her heart, and at the moment she didn't think it would ever mend.

Nettie tugged at her shawl and searched for the right words to hurl at him.

"I'm sorry, Nettie. What I said was wrong."

The apology came too late. "It doesn't matter," she said. "No matter what we say and pretend, this marriage is a mockery."

"Are you saying you don't love me?" He looked cold, hard—not the Riley she'd grown to care for.

She wouldn't let him use her love against her. She'd seen what happened when a woman loved a man too much. Her parents were the best examples. Only in the end did her father truly love Nettie's mother for sticking by him all those years.

"As I said, it doesn't matter," Nettie said.

Not a muscle moved on his rugged features. He moved past her into the soddie. "I'm leaving," he said. "I'm getting my things and heading back to Montana where I belong."

"Fine with me. I've neglected my temperance work anyway."

She watched his broad shoulders stiffen. How she wanted to call after him, to tell him she loved him with all her heart. He'd come into her life as a blessing when her world lay in shambles. Only the Lord took precedence over him. She knew one word from her, and he'd turn and listen.

She needed to apologize, but she couldn't go to Montana, not with a baby coming next May.

Before she and Riley realized their love, she'd clung to her friends and family. Leaving them meant saying farewell to those she'd always cherish, but Riley's baby meant more. If she went with him, she'd jeopardize the life of his child, but she refused to keep him in Mesquite because of his baby. She'd planned on telling him the news that night, and they could prepare all winter for this dear gift. She wanted to knit tiny clothes, talk about names, and dream about a treasure of a baby with Riley's blue eyes. Not watch Riley ride away.

Nettie refused to shed one more tear for her husband. Riley or their child, what a horrible choice to make.

She needed a good midwife to help her. Riley said Montana held few women, and what did he know about birthing babies? She'd been a midwife, and, even so, the thought of giving birth alone frightened her. Maybe she knew too much about what could go wrong. And because of her decision to live alone in Mesquite and bear his child, she said nothing, not even a good-bye when he rode out. He thought she didn't love him, and she'd been too stubborn to tell him otherwise.

❧

The despair of the world rested on Riley's heart and mind. Even when he'd stayed drunk, his low thoughts had been about his own stupidity. No one else had been involved. This pain was different. It felt like someone had stabbed him and twisted the knife. All this time he thought Nettie loved him as he loved her. Now he better understood why she refused to move to Montana. She had her friends here, a compensation for a loveless marriage.

Nettie had lied to him. She'd said she loved him many times. Even in her sleep he heard her whisper those endearing words. Riley couldn't stay here another day, not with the hurt scratching at his heart and telling him he was a fool. How clever his wife. He wished he despised her, but he couldn't—not yet anyway.

Riding back to Mesquite had brought one mistake after another. At least he'd found Abe and thanked him properly for all his goodness. He'd tell him good-bye before moving toward Montana. The old man would want to pray with him, probably try to change his mind about Nettie. He'd have liked to take Abe with him, but the old man had already made it clear where he wanted to meet Jesus. What was it about this hard land that drove folks to stay no matter what?

Sooner than he realized, Riley caught sight of Abe's place. He considered not telling him about the trouble with Nettie, but the old man had keen perception. No point hiding the truth.

"Good to see you, Riley." Abe hobbled from his house as though every bone in his body ached. "Hadn't expected you this early in the week. Are you all right? You look a mite poorly."

Riley leaned on his saddle horn. He patted his chestnut

mare. "I've come to say I'm leaving for Montana."

"Well, I'm sorry. I'll miss Nettie."

"She isn't going."

Abe simply stared at him. "I should have been able to see the misery on your face. You two have a spat?"

Riley clenched his jaw. "Reckon so. We had an argument about moving to Montana, and in the heat of things she let me know she didn't care about me."

Abe pursed his lips together. "I think you're wrong, Son. Nettie is devoted to you; I've seen it in her eyes and heard it in her voice."

"When I asked her, she said it didn't matter."

"I'm sorry, real sorry, 'specially since I encouraged you about honoring your marriage." Abe peered up at him. "Guess I should have stayed out of it."

"Naw, Abe. I don't blame you. You were simply following what the Bible says about promises. I care about Nettie a lot, but I don't want to be a nuisance."

"So you're moving on."

Riley picked up his reins. "Yeah, and I'll write. I'll also be praying for Frank and his family. Sure is a shame about that son of yours. I still believe if God can do a mighty work in me, then He can do even more with Frank."

"Thank you. God bless you, Riley. I wish you the best, and I'll be praying you and Nettie work out your differences. Perhaps the time away from each other will give both of you answers."

Riley forced a grim smile, but he didn't reply. If he talked to Abe much longer, he'd be crying like a baby. Without another word, he spurred his mare on, leaving behind his memories and carrying his broken dreams.

Riley avoided Mesquite. What few supplies he needed could be purchased in the next town. With his luck, the judge might be in a mood to throw him in jail again. His thoughts focused on Preacher Faulkner. The man deserved an explanation as to why he left Nettie, and he'd get one as soon as Riley made it back to Montana. Maybe Maudie Mae and Nettie could resume their friendship.

Riley took a deep breath and brushed a lone tear rolling down his cheek. If he couldn't be with his wife to love her proper, he'd send enough money so she wouldn't want for anything.

Lord, is this how You want life for me? Living alone without my wife? I'm confused and wondering what I did wrong. Is it all because I agreed to marry Nettie without consulting You like I should? I love her, Lord. It will take a long time to get over her—maybe I never will. Take care of her, please. She loves You. It's me she doesn't want in her life.

twelve

The following days were more difficult than Nettie could have ever imagined. She remembered caring for her ill parents and learning the duties of a midwife, but the emptiness in her heart far exceeded those times of exhaustion. Long days and even longer nights left her in tears most of the time. She wanted to attribute her moodiness to the baby, but she missed Riley. She repeatedly recalled the conversation the day he left, wishing she hadn't been so stubborn. She asked God's forgiveness, but she didn't know how to contact Riley.

Nettie loved him, and he needed to hear those words from her lips. Many times she had anticipated his joy at learning they were going to have a baby. If she'd been honest, he'd have understood her reluctance to move to Montana with a child on the way. The thought of leaving her friends frightened her, but those problems could have been worked out. Riley might have even decided to sell his ranch and make a home in Nebraska. So many things could have been done differently, but instead, she'd acted as though he were a nuisance instead of the husband she adored.

Many women experienced morning sickness, but not Nettie. For that consideration, she was thankful. She drank red raspberry tea and ate regularly. As the time passed, she knitted and sewed tiny clothes and wished Riley sat in front of the fireplace beside her. They used to watch the flames dance, and the sight always put a story into his head, and he told the best she'd ever heard. She could listen to him for hours. Oh, she missed that man.

Nettie couldn't avoid folks forever, but as long as the cold weather persisted, she could hide the babe. When the snows melted and spring arrived, she'd be much too big to hide the truth from anyone.

"For a woman grieving the loss of her husband, something must be appealing to you 'cause you're filling out," Maudie Mae said during an unannounced visit. She looked down her long nose and studied Nettie.

"Do you think so?" Nettie's hands trembled. At her feet lay the basket of knitting.

"Why, yes, the bosom of your dress is tight."

Nettie reddened and immediately she covered her chest. "My. . .my mother was a bit portly. Possibly I'm becoming more like her."

"Possibly," Maudie Mae said. "Is there something you're not telling me?"

Nettie's heart hammered furiously, but she remained unmoved in her stand. "What could that possibly be?"

"I'm not sure, but I believe you are."

When Nettie offered nothing more, Maudie Mae reached into her pocket and retrieved a letter. "This came for you, and I thought I'd bring it. I was at the store when it came in on the stage." She handed it to Nettie. "Looks like it's from Riley."

Irritation crept over her bones. Riley's letter was none of Maudie Mae's concern.

"Aren't you going to open it?" Maudie Mae asked.

"I will later."

"Humph. You mean when I'm not around."

Nettie knew her friend was miffed, but the days of Maudie Mae telling her what to do were over. She loved her friend, but the affection didn't rule over priorities—and Riley's words were definitely a priority. Nettie reached over to take Maudie Mae's hand. "I'm sorry, but this is private. You understand, don't you?"

"I suppose. Why isn't he here? Couldn't take him all this time to tend to business in Montana."

"Winter snows have most likely kept him inside. I'm sure his letter will explain everything."

Maudie Mae studied her. "I must be getting back to town. I saw snow clouds on my way here, and I don't want to be caught in the middle of a storm."

"Of course. No point in worrying the judge. Would you give Preacher Faulkner my best? He's such a dear man."

Maudie Mae agreed. "Thank you for the coffee, and now I'll be on my way." She walked to the door, and Nettie breathed a sigh of relief. Her friend arranged her coat and scarf, then glanced about the room. Her gaze fell upon the knitting basket. Instantly she walked to the chair and knelt beside it. The knitting fell between her fingers. "Nettie O'Connor, you're carrying a baby."

Nettie moistened her lips and didn't say a word.

"You are!" Maudie Mae's voice rang triumphantly, then she immediately sobered. "Riley doesn't know, does he?"

The tears started to fall, but Nettie blinked them back. She didn't want to lie, and she didn't want to admit the truth. The baby was her precious secret.

"Nettie?" Maudie Mae replaced the knitting and stood. She touched Nettie's cheek. "This is supposed to be a happy time, not filled with sadness."

Those words broke Nettie's carefully guarded emotions, and a river of despair ran down her cheeks. Maudie Mae pulled her into an embrace.

"Riley isn't coming back, is he?" her friend asked.

The truth shook Nettie's heart. "I don't know for sure."

"And he doesn't know about the baby?"

Nettie could only stare at Maudie Mae. "I don't want him to come home because of the baby, but because he loves me."

"I thought he told you he did."

"Maudie Mae, he did many times. It was me who said ugly things." Nettie proceeded to tell Maudie Mae the entire story.

"A man deserves to know about his child." Maudie Mae pointed her finger at Nettie.

"I agree, but right now I'm not sure how to tell Riley anything." She lifted the letter in her hand. "This missive is the first I've heard from him."

"I'm sure he's grieving because he's not here with you, and Christmas will be here in another week." Maude Mae pulled off her glove and wiped away Nettie's tears. "I'm your friend, and I'm going to help you through this."

Nettie swallowed and attempted to smile. "Thank you. I think I need to keep busy."

"Probably so. Are you still interested in visiting Mrs. Wilkins and her daughter?"

"Yes. I've been taking them food now and then."

"Good, we can do it together. Perhaps we could begin Sunday after church, providing the weather is fitting."

"I'd like that." Already Nettie felt better.

Maudie Mae lifted her chin. "For now, I'm leaving so you can read Riley's letter. Maybe he's changed his mind."

"A lovely thought," Nettie said, but she doubted its veracity.

After Maudie Mae left, Nettie poured another cup of coffee and sat in front of the fire with Riley's letter. She wanted to savor every word, but fear of its contents stopped her.

Oh Lord, if the news is bad, I don't know what I'll do. Give me the strength to be the woman You want me to be. Nettie touched her stomach. She hadn't thanked God for the wee babe inside her. *And Lord, thank You for this baby. I'll be a good mother and bring up him or her knowing You.*

Nettie carefully opened the letter and began to read.

Dear Nettie,

I pray this letter finds you well and happy. My thoughts linger on you when I wake in the morning and before I fall asleep. Only the good Lord takes more of my time.

Winter has set in hard here in Montana. The snow is waist deep in most places, and it's a wondrous sight. I do enjoy seeing the animal prints—but not wolves—across the white blanket. Reminds me of how God forgives us for all we do, even when we sin again. I feel like those tracks, Nettie. I ask forgiveness, the Lord wipes my life clean, and then I sin again. My sins have followed me all the way from Nebraska. I shouldn't have left you that way. We should have talked and figured out something besides me riding off angry. I'm surrounded by all of the things I love, but nothing compares with how much I love and miss you. I know you don't have feelings for me. Even so, it doesn't change my heart. Do you have any idea how many times I wish I'd turned around and asked for another chance?

I was thinking about how you and I used to sit and watch the fire, and then out of nowhere, I'd come up with a story. You always laughed and made a fuss no matter how ridiculous I sounded. You made me feel real special, and I miss it. Now, whenever I look into the fire, all I can see is your sweet face. Did anybody ever tell you that you have the most beautiful gray eyes?

The Lord's been a good companion. He's constantly bringing Scripture to mind that I can use and think on. I've been talking to Sam, my foreman, for a long time about Jesus, and lately he's started to ask questions.

Have you heard from Abe? I rode over to his place the day I left. He told me he would check in on you. He's mighty frail looking. I hope he makes it through the winter. I keep praying for him and Frank.

Here's a little money to help you through the lean times. Don't be getting mad, Nettie. I want you to have it.

All my devotion,
Riley

The baby kicked just as she folded the letter. Nettie held her hand on her stomach and laughed lightly. New life brought such joy. Tonight she'd write to Riley. She must tell him she loved him and wanted his forgiveness. She dared not tell him about the baby, not yet. Once their little guest found his way into the world, she'd go to Riley in Montana. She'd do whatever it took to work out their problems.

❧

Riley's mare stumbled through the snow. A few head of cattle had drifted away, and he wanted them down from the hills before they froze to death. The wind blew sharp around his face, and he pulled his woolen scarf over his mouth. The biting cold seemed to settle in his bones, but warm thoughts of Nettie kept him moving on. Today, like every day for the past two weeks, he recalled every word of Nettie's letter.

Dearest Riley,

I've tried three times to begin this letter, and each time the words all ran together like the sorghum you used to pour over your corn bread. I love you, Riley. I never stopped loving you. Please forgive me for not telling you this before you rode out. I never thought I could love anyone like I do you. If you still want me, I'll come to Montana when spring arrives. Nothing is more important than being with you. I pray it's not too late.

I've been taking food to Frank's wife when the weather is fitting, and today Maudie Mae suggested we do it together. Mrs. Wilkins is not a believer, but she has been coming to church. Abe stops by regular. We talk, then I fix him something to eat, then we talk some more. He looks a little older each time I see him, but I believe he won't give up this life until Frank finds Jesus.

Excuse me, I've been writing on and on about me and have not inquired about you. Are you eating properly and keeping warm? And what of Sam? I've been praying for him. In fact, I've been praying for all of your hired hands. How are your horses and cows faring in this cold?

Christmas will be here soon, and I pray the next one and

*the many holidays afterward will find us together—loving
each other as God intended.*

*Fondest regards,
Nettie*

Riley had been so happy when he got that letter that a couple of his hands had wondered if he'd been drinking.

"I gave the devil's brew up a long time ago. I got a letter from my wife in Nebraska, and she's planning to come in the spring," Riley said. He glanced from the barn to the house, where his cook had a roaring fire. The mere notion of Nettie inside that house made him feel like a kid again.

"If she makes you this happy, then maybe you need to go after her," Sam said.

Riley grinned. Maybe his friend had a good idea. After chores and supper, he sat down with his dog at his feet and penned his reply.

My dearest Nettie,

I hope you haven't changed your mind, because I'm counting the days until spring. A husband and wife need to be together, and I know whatever problems we had can be worked out with God's help.

I hope you weren't alone at Christmas. The nearest church was too far to travel to in the snow, so I did my best at getting the hands to listen to the Christmas story from the Bible. The cook fixed us a fine meal, and we had a good celebration, but my heart kept drifting back to Nebraska.

You asked about my hired hands. I have Sam and four others. One of the men is about to get married, so that will be good womenfolk company for you. You'll love this country, especially in the spring when the valley is bursting in green and the many colors of wildflowers. We even have goldenrod here.

I don't want to think of you making the trip from Nebraska here by yourself. When the weather breaks, I'll be heading your way. We'll have a lot of time to talk on the way back.

All my devotion,
Riley

A month later, Riley received a second letter from Nettie.

My wonderful husband,

I'm so excited about seeing you. Winter winds are blowing around the soddie, and snow is drifting on the north side, but my heart is warm with thoughts of you and dreams of our life together. Never will I let you leave me again. I'll simply tie a rope around my waist and hook it in your belt.

I too have been spending a great deal of time in God's Word. He has shown me how incredibly selfish I am. Again, I ask your forgiveness. I promise I will do my best to be the best wife in Montana—even in the whole United States. God knows I'm a bit stubborn, but he's given me Scripture after Scripture to memorize.

Celia Wilkins and her daughter Mary prayed to receive Christ today. I cried like a baby. Nothing has changed with Frank, but now two more people are praying for him. Abe has been doctoring a bad cold all winter. Riley, I worry about him. He says Jesus is coming for him soon. I hope, for your sake, he doesn't go until spring. We talk about you every time we're together. He thinks of you as a son.

The judge stuck Frank in jail for his drinking. Maudie Mae said he refused to pay his bill at the saloon, and it made the judge powerful mad. At least in jail, Frank can't drink. Preacher Faulkner and Abe went to see him, but I don't know what happened.

When you come for me in the spring, I have so much more to tell you. Do you know when? I'm so anxious. Do be careful and take care of yourself.

Your most devoted wife,
Nettie

thirteen

Nettie thought she'd go to her grave with a backache. Seven months' pregnant, and she felt like a walking soddie. Driving the wagon into Mesquite for Sunday church made her back throb, then she spent a grueling morning in church. To make matters worse, Maudie Mae suggested the ladies involved with the temperance movement meet at her home following a church dinner, complete with chicken, vegetables, corn bread, and dried fruit cobblers. All Nettie wanted to do was sleep, and of course that wasn't possible until she drove the wagon home after the meeting.

Maudie Mae and the judge were the only folks in town who had a home built entirely of wood. The boardinghouse also held the distinction, but according to Maudie Mae, a proprietorship wasn't a real home. The stately whitewashed, clapboard home with its wide front porch and many long windows on both the first and second floors nearly took Nettie's breath away each time she saw it.

The Balshes' house also had a parlor, the site of many ladies' meetings. Maudie Mae had furnished the room in deep green velvet with many chairs and an elegant sofa. Layers of thick drapes covered the windows so the sunlight didn't fade the furniture and gold-striped wallpaper, but it made the room dark, especially with the walnut furniture. She always let her callers know the furniture had been shipped all the way from New York City. The walls held many pictures and mirrors, and on the tables sat more pictures and Maudie Mae's special treasures. The parlor always looked crowded, even before anyone entered.

This afternoon Nettie sat stiffly on a prized settee in an effort to focus her attention on the ladies who chatted about the latest gossip, their children, and Preacher Faulkner's sermon.

"Let's all come to order." Maude Mae stood to address the small group. She had a way of looking down her pointed nose that made a person snap to attention. Everyone knew her good heart, and the immediate fear dissipated with a smile she willingly bestowed. "We have a new face with us today." She nodded in Celia Wilkins's direction. "I want all of you to properly welcome Celia Wilkins."

The ladies clapped, and Celia blushed.

"We're so glad you have joined us," Maudie Mae said, "and even more grateful that you have found the Lord."

Again, the ladies applauded. Nettie joined in to keep from falling asleep. Granted, she cared very much for Celia and her daughter Mary, although she'd care more after a hearty nap.

"Who would like to open our gathering in a word of prayer?" Maudie Mae asked. When no one responded, she bowed her head. "Heavenly Father, we thank Thee for the opportunity to meet together on this beautiful Sunday. We ask Thee to bless our meeting and show us how to guide the people of Mesquite away from the evils of alcohol. In Jesus' name, amen."

Maudie Mae remained standing and spread her arms as though she wished to embrace them all. Nettie stifled a giggle, but not so long ago, she'd been just as demonstrative. "Ladies, what have we to report on our work?"

The woman who owned the boardinghouse with her husband stood and glanced about nervously. "When my husband suggested we serve whiskey with our meals, I promptly told him no."

Everyone clapped for several minutes until she lowered herself into an overstuffed chair.

"I'd like to organize another hymn sing in front of the saloon," Maudie Mae said. "As long as we don't block the door, my husband can't complain."

The other ladies nodded in agreement.

"We could do this next Saturday afternoon, say around four o'clock?"

The date and time settled, Maudie Mae clasped her hands in front of her. "Does anyone have anything to add to our meeting?"

Nettie took several long moments to rise to her feet. Her swollen ankles felt like tree trunks. She'd put off telling the others her thoughts for long enough. "I do have a few things to say." She peered into each lady's face. "First of all, I want you to understand that I care very deeply about the temperance movement, and nothing has changed regarding my sentiments. As you well know, in the past I was the first to volunteer in any endeavor that might dissuade the people of our town from drinking. I'm sure none of you have forgotten my period of incarceration when I marched into the saloon and preached what I thought was a message from God, then dumped a man's drink on the floor."

The ladies fanned themselves.

"I thank you for all of your visits."

No one said a word, since Maudie Mae and Preacher Faulkner were the only two people in town who went to see Nettie in jail.

"While I was there, in addition to meeting Riley and marrying him, I heard some profound words of wisdom from Preacher Faulkner."

"Pray tell, Sister, what were they? We want to know," Maudie Mae asked. She took a seat and studied Nettie, as though she hadn't heard the preacher's words.

"He suggested that from my heart I give to those who patronize the saloon the same love our Lord gives us. Preacher Faulkner believes we can do more to help our movement with kindness than with condemnation."

One of the ladies, an older widow, stiffened. "Nettie O'Connor, you are wrong. Those drunks need to hear what is going to happen to them if they continue in their evil ways.

Shout it from the rooftops, I say. Fire and brimstone are the destination for those who choose the path of strong drink."

"I agree," another woman said. "Those whiskey-drinking fools smell badly and look worse."

Maudie Mae shifted uncomfortably. Nettie wondered if those ladies remembered the judge owned the saloon. And Celia, how did this make her feel?

"Shall we conduct ourselves as ladies?" Maudie Mae asked.

Nettie took a deep breath. "Please, ladies, hear me out before you pass judgment. With the preacher's suggestion, I started taking meals to the women who work at the saloon. One of those women has been attending church. I don't think she would have done so without seeing Christian charity. I'm not saying this to boast, but to show you what God has done through me—in spite of me. Another very young woman who worked at the saloon has contacted her family in Lincoln, and they have sent her money to come home."

A hush fell in Maudie Mae's parlor.

"I'm not suggesting any of you stop singing hymns outside the saloon or any of the other measures you feel God has directed. What I do want you to know is I have found a way that has brought two women closer to finding meaning and purpose in their lives, and I will continue."

"Make that three women." Celia Wilkins stood, and with a deep breath and tears rolling down her cheeks, she said, "Nettie and later Maudie Mae started bringing food to me and my daughter. You all know Frank drinks all our money away unless I can get some of it while he's passed-out drunk. Maudie Mae and Nettie didn't condemn me or tell me I wasn't a good wife, but they loved me and talked to me about Jesus. They brought food and a coat for my Mary. If not for my dear, new friends, I would not have started attending church with my daughter, and I would not have come to God's saving grace. Frank is still the same, but now I have hope." She lifted a tear-glazed smile to Nettie, then to Maudie Mae. "Thank you. I am forever indebted."

Someone handed Celia a handkerchief. She dabbed at her eyes, then resumed her position on an overstuffed chair.

Maudie Mae stood and visibly found it difficult to maintain her composure. "I believe Nettie and Celia have shown us our God can and will move us in the direction He desires. We. . .we need to make sure we seek His direction before we act."

The ladies applauded, even the two who had objected to Nettie and Maudie Mae's methods. All of them smiled through misty eyes. Nettie wiped her dampened cheeks and sat down. Her back still ached, but she felt good inside, and the pain no longer mattered. All the way home, she thought about the afternoon with Maudie Mae. She couldn't wait to write Riley and tell him all about it.

Nettie really missed Riley, and she prayed for a quick spring in the mountains. In the next breath, she realized if he didn't get there soon, she'd hitch up the wagon and drive to Montana by herself. She might even deliver their baby along the way.

❧

"What are you doing out here in this cold?" Sam asked Riley. A blast of wind nearly knocked both men down.

"I was looking to do a few repairs on the house," Riley said, shaking a loose piece of wood. The wind always did a fair amount of damage to the buildings.

"Now? Why it's nearly zero out here."

Riley could barely hear him above the roar of the wind. "I don't want to be stuck here in the spring when I could be heading to Nebraska."

Sam laughed. "Riley, I'll make the repairs if you don't get them done in time. You aren't going to do your wife a bit of good with frostbite."

Riley knew Sam made a lot of sense. "I want the ranch to look its best. And I know Nettie will want to put up curtains and all those other womenfolk things, but I don't want her to find the house in bad shape."

"She won't," Sam said. "Like I said, me and the boys will have this place looking like one of those fancy homes back East."

Riley sucked in a cold breath. "I can't say no to that."

A short while later, the two warmed themselves inside by the fire.

"Just how pretty is your wife?" Sam asked with a grin. "I want to be prepared if she looks like one of our cows."

Riley roared. "I wish I had a picture. Nettie has dark, nearly black, silky hair and the biggest gray eyes I've ever seen. Her skin is smooth and her cheeks look like a peach kissed 'em. And she's not a big woman, not at all."

"Close to perfect?"

"Hmm. Perfect for me. She does have a bit of a temper now and then, but a different opinion makes life interesting."

"Tell me, what does a pretty woman see in you?" Sam slapped him on the back.

Both men wrapped their hands around a hot mug of coffee.

"I've been called a dandy in my day," Riley said.

"Not around here, unless you're claiming kin to some of those wolves we've been fighting off the cattle."

"You," Riley said, "are jealous because I've got me a wife." He chuckled.

"Ah, maybe a little. Do you think if I put the Lord first in my life like you, He'd give me a good woman to marry up?" Sam asked.

Riley thought on his words. "I believe if you give Him your life, it won't matter whether you have a wife or not. The Lord is enough to fill all our needs."

Sam rubbed the back of his neck, then took a gulp of the coffee. "I see. It gets kind of lonesome out here sometimes. You've been a good friend, but now that your wife is coming. . . well, I thought I'd like to have one too."

Riley placed a hand on Sam's shoulder. "You turn all of those worries over to the Lord, and He'll take care of them better than you ever thought possible."

Sam hesitated. "I've been thinking on Jesus, thinking real hard."

"When you're ready, I'll pray with you."

Sam rubbed his neck again. "I believe I'm ready now."

Thankfulness to God swelled in Riley's heart. He grabbed his friend's shoulder. "The angels will be celebratin' tonight." With the flames of a roaring fire spitting and crackling, Riley led Sam to heaven's gateway. "Lord, Sam here is asking You to forgive his sins and guide his life. I've talked to him about Your Son, Jesus. I told him how You loved us enough to send Your Son to the cross so we can one day live with You. Through Your grace and mercy, make Your home in Sam's heart just like You've done in mine. He wants to walk with You for the rest of his life, amen."

❧

"Isn't his news wonderful?" Nettie asked Abe. She folded up Riley's letter and slipped it into her dress pocket. "And it all started with you helping a man broken and beat up."

Abe chuckled. "It was all the Lord. I simply did what He asked of me."

Nettie recalled Celia and the young woman already living back in Lincoln with her parents. "I wish I had listened sooner instead of being so stubborn. I'm so proud of my husband. He's a gem for sure."

"I think both of you are refined gold."

Nettie patted his thin hand. "Each time I leave you, I tell myself I'm going to remember all of your words of wisdom. I best start bringing paper."

"For this dried-up old man?"

"Yes, a man I dearly love."

"I didn't always walk this close with the Lord. Sometimes I think Frank is so set in his ways because of me. I used to carry on like him until he was about six years old. That's when I found the Lord."

Nettie's heart nearly broke with his sad words. "Oh, Abe. Your past has nothing to do with Frank. He's free to make his own choices. If anything at all, he should see your goodness."

"I keep praying for a change. I just have to hold on to God's hand and take each day as it happens."

"That's all any of us can do." Nettie saw he looked tired. "You need to rest. I don't think you take good enough care of yourself."

Abe closed his eyes. "You sure are one to talk, traipsing out here in the cold when you're so sleepy, your pretty eyes droop."

Nettie laughed. "I do sleep a lot. Good thing it's winter and there's not much work. Sometimes I think I'm kin to a bear."

"A right pretty bear, I might add." Abe laughed and folded his hands in his lap. "Have you told Riley about the baby?"

Guilt tingled from the top of her head to her toes. "No. Every time I think I will, something stops me, most likely myself."

"Little Mama, what are you afraid of?"

She rested her head back on the chair. A hundred thoughts raced across her mind, and Riley rode every one of them. "I want him to want me as his wife, not put up with me because I'm having his baby."

"You know better," Abe said. "He loves you with or without the babe."

Nettie felt the baby kick with his words, as though making sure she listened to Abe's wisdom. "I hope so. I dearly hope so."

fourteen

Riley stuffed an extra shirt inside his saddlebag. Next he added his Bible. He'd finished packing what he needed for the journey to Mesquite. Winter snows still threatened, but April brought less of a likelihood of blizzards. He could skirt around the mountainous areas, which often brought several feet of snow well into May. Besides Riley couldn't stay in Montana any longer; his wife waited for his arrival in Mesquite.

Snatching up a mug of coffee, he downed it in one gulp. His cook made a great pot, but for the next couple of weeks, he'd be forced to drink his own pathetic brew. Riley gathered up his saddlebags and headed for the barn. The air felt crisp but without the bitter cold from the past several months. These temperatures merely filled him with vigor, like a frisky new colt. Foot-long icicles dripped from the roofs and overhangs of the house and outbuildings in the sparkling morning sun, while the streams took on a thinner look, and some gurgled free. It wouldn't be long before he'd be able to sneak off with his fishing pole. He wondered if Nettie liked fishing.

Glancing in all directions at the beauty of God's handiwork, Riley took a few moments to breathe in the air enveloping his land. The clear blue sky contrasted with the white snow and evergreens in the distance. Once more, he imagined Nettie's response to this beautiful territory.

He thought about waking up in the morning with his sweet wife beside him. When he got her there with him, he intended to take care of her good and proper for as long as the good Lord gave him life.

"Are you sure you need to venture out toward Nebrasky?"

Sam asked. He quickly picked up pace with Riley. "There's more bad weather yet in these parts."

With the snow crunching beneath his feet, Riley continued to move on to the barn. "I don't think we'll get any more heavy storms, but I do expect a few squalls."

"Be prepared for a lot," Sam said. "Have you forgotten past springs?"

Riley hadn't forgotten anything about Montana snowfall. Rather, he chose to shove the temperamental weather aside and ponder his future with Nettie. "It would take more than battling a little snow to keep me from being with my wife."

"I'm sure she'd prefer a live man rather than one froze to death."

Riley chuckled. "I'll be fine and back here before you know it. I'm expecting a good many calves in late spring, and several of the mares are due too. All the more reason why I need to leave now and get back."

"Suit yourself, but I'll be praying for you."

Sam's last words touched him. How good to know his friend now had a home in heaven. "Thanks." He shook Sam's hand before lifting the latch on the barn. "I have to take care of myself. Who else would you have to bother?"

Riley saddled his mare and headed in a southerly direction toward Billings. From there he planned to ride east to the South Dakota border, then head south into Wyoming and out across to Nebraska. Some of the riding might be a bit rough, but Riley didn't care. He had his sights on Nettie.

North of the Crow Reservation in Montana, he stopped one evening to make camp. Riley soon had a fire going, and the smell of wood plus the fire's spits and crackles made him warm and sleepy. He awoke to dying embers and the sound of something thrashing in the trees behind him. His mare screamed. Riley snatched up his rifle and added more wood to the fire. The last thing he needed was a hungry bear fresh out of hibernation.

He glanced into the fire and prayed for the flames to lap up the wood and dance high enough to light up the night. The thrashing continued. With his rifle in one hand, Riley moved toward his horse tethered close by.

"Easy, Lady." The sound of his voice calmed the mare for only a moment. A bear roared, its angry bellow awakening the forest.

Riley stepped back with his finger resting a hair-span from the rifle's trigger. *Lord, I'm not ready to die. Help me!*

The huge animal stepped into the campsite, its muscle-laden features lit up by the flames that once meant comfort. The bear opened its mouth, like the black heat of a black-smith's forge. Riley raised the rifle, but the bear swung at the barrel and knocked it from his grasp. The bear advanced and swiped at him. Its claws scraped down Riley's left arm. He slipped and fell on top of his rifle. Scooting backwards, Riley wound his fingers around the weapon and pulled it to aim again. In the precious few seconds he had to consider his fate, Riley aimed at the grizzly's neck and fired. The animal reared back, angry, hurt. Ignoring the pain in his arm, he aimed just below the bear's ear lobe, all the while praying the bullet met its target. The bear roared and stumbled. Riley took aim and fired again into the animal's neck.

With what sounded like a tree crashing onto the forest floor, the grizzly fell backwards. Riley sunk two more shots into the animal before making his way back to his saddlebag. He hadn't intended for his spare shirt to bind the wounds caused by a grizzly. Pulling out the shirt with his right hand, he attempted to calculate how much blood he'd lost. From his shoulder to below his elbow lay open flesh. Wrapping the wound the best he could, Riley realized he needed a doctor and fast. Leaning back with his head on his saddle and his right arm clutched to his left, he decided to wait until dawn, then head into the Crow Indian Reservation. He hoped the Indians didn't hate the sight of a white man enough to let him bleed to death.

Riley was long overdue. Nettie had calculated he'd arrive by mid-April, but it had been two weeks since then. Where could he be? Had he left too soon and got caught in some mountain blizzard? Nettie shuddered. She didn't want to consider something terrible stopping Riley from getting to Mesquite.

To make matters worse, Abe hadn't been able to recover from the winter cold. He had a harsh cough that seemed to roar from his toes. Nothing soothed it, and fever and chills came and left without warning. She'd administered ginger tea and feverfew for the headache, and they helped for a little while. Preacher Faulkner said Abe wasn't for this world much longer. She'd talked to Celia about Frank visiting his father, but the man refused. Poor Abe. All he'd ever wanted was for his son to trust in the Lord instead of a bottle of whiskey.

Soon Nettie would enter her ninth month of pregnancy. She'd never felt this miserable in her life. Her ankles swelled so badly that some days she couldn't wear her shoes. Lacing them up proved nearly impossible. She remembered the times Riley told her she was pretty. He'd change his tune at his first glimpse of her. She hoped her enlarged body didn't send him right back to Montana. Nothing about her resembled beauty.

Over the winter she'd sewn and knitted tiny clothes and blankets for the baby, more than she'd probably ever need. Now as the time grew closer, she contemplated names. First she liked this one, then another. When so many of them rolled around in her head, she chose to wait until she and Riley saw what the baby looked like. Nettie didn't care if it were a boy or girl, just as long as it was a strong, healthy baby.

Nettie took the bucket to the well. The days of midwife duties broke her thoughts too many times of late. Mostly she recalled the nightmare tales when a mother died or when both the mother and wee babe didn't survive childbirth. She'd spoken to Mesquite's midwife on occasion, and the woman seemed knowledgeable. But if Riley didn't arrive home soon, who would summon her? What if Nettie went into labor alone before Riley returned?

Drawing up the water, Nettie carried it inside so she could make fresh coffee when Maudie Mae arrived. Her friend always eased her doubts and worries with the latest news from among the womenfolk. Last week, she'd brought Celia with her, and they'd ridden over to see Abe. Having three women call brightened Abe's spirits.

"Nettie, you look ready to explode like a kernel of popcorn," Maudie Mae said. "And pardon me for saying so, but your baby has to weigh ten pounds."

Nettie shivered. "Don't say that. Scares me to death."

Maudie Mae reached over to pat her hand in the familiar, soothing way. "I'm only teasing. Don't pay any attention to me."

"But I am big, and I'm afraid this baby will want to be born before Riley gets here." Huge tears pooled in Nettie's eyes. She picked up a handkerchief. "Look at me, crying over every other word. I should be ashamed."

"You're wanting this child to get here, that's all. Believe me, the births after the first one are much easier."

Nettie continued to weep. "Once this one gets here, I might never have another."

"Of course you will. You've helped through enough births to know the pain is quickly forgotten in light of the new baby," Maudie Mae said. "I well remember my children's arrivals, but I don't remember the pain of getting them here."

"It's Riley I'm concerned about," Nettie said. "He should have been here by now."

Maudie Mae moistened her lips. "He'll get here in time. He might be here this very night."

"What if something bad happened to him? He might be lying sick or injured somewhere." Nettie peered into Maudie Mae's face for reassurance.

"Nonsense. I do have a request though. Why not move into the boardinghouse while you wait for the baby? I can keep an eye on you until Riley arrives."

Nettie sobered and nodded. "I've considered as such, so maybe I should take your advice."

"If it makes you feel any better, I'll wire near where he lives."

Nettie smiled. "Thank you. Yes, that would make me feel better." *And please, tell me my husband is all right.*

❧

Riley fought to awaken from a haze of pain. He must wake up and ride into the reservation. His arm needed doctoring. The grizzly might not be dead. Nettie expected him.

"Mr. O'Connor. Mr. O'Connor." A man's voice seized his attention. It sounded like it came from the bottom of a deep well. Riley struggled to respond.

"He's stirrin'," a woman said. "Sir, you need to open your eyes."

Riley's eyelids felt nailed together. How did this happen? The male voice called to him again. This time Riley tried to speak. He could move his lips, but no utterances came.

"He's wantin' to talk," the woman said.

Riley mustered all the strength he could and willed his eyes to open, first a slit of light, then a fog of faces. At last he focused on two people who stared at him anxiously.

"I see you have decided to join us," the man said, his kind eyes radiating concern. "You gave us quite a scare, but you're doing much better."

"The grizzly," Riley said.

"We heard about the bear from our friends among the Crow Indians."

Riley blinked to pay attention to the stranger—a man with a mottled gray beard.

"I'm Doc Foreman, and this is my wife, Judith. A couple of braves brought you to us day before yesterday. You looked more dead than alive, but I think you're going to make it. We went through your saddlebags and found out your name. Hope you don't mind."

Riley found it nearly impossible to speak. Nettie, he had to get word to her that he'd be late. "My. . .my arm."

"It will heal," Doc Foreman said. "You're one lucky man to live through the mauling of a bear and the loss of blood."

He wasn't lucky, simply blessed. When Riley felt better, he'd explain that to the doc.

"I'm going to have my wife feed you a little broth. You need your strength."

Judith Foreman touched his cheek. She was a bone-thin woman with the same kind eyes and a gentle touch. "I have it ready, Mr. O'Connor. Try to help me while I spoon it in. We've been praying for you, and I believe the good Lord is smiling your way."

Believers. Thank You, Lord.

Riley did try, but the effort to open his mouth proved to be one of the most difficult things he'd ever done. At first the broth trickled over his chin, but Mrs. Foreman held his mouth open while spooning in the warm liquid. It tasted good as it dribbled down his throat. He needed this, lots of this, to get well.

Two days later, Riley's weak body forced him to stay in bed while his mind told him to climb out of there and move on. The combination left him cranky.

"I see you're feeling better," Mrs. Foreman said. "Your feisty attitude is wanting to bubble over."

"I want to get to my wife," Riley said. "I'm grateful for all you and your husband have done—"

"Don't forget the Crows."

"Them too for taking care of me, but you don't understand. I haven't seen my wife for nearly seven months, and she'll be worried."

"You're starting to get up and about. Soon you'll be riding out of here."

"Not soon enough," he said and closed his eyes. *Oh, Lord, don't let Nettie worry about me, and please heal this body fast. I'm grateful for You sparing my life, really I am.*

Five days later, Riley thanked the Foremans and their Crow friends properly before riding on again. He'd learned the Foreman's faith had led them to the reservation to do whatever necessary in aiding the Indians. Riley promised to send payment to the doctor and his wife and have his men drive a few cows to the Indians. None of them had asked for anything, but Riley believed in paying his debts.

The miles ahead were certain to be slow, but at least he could put them behind him. He found his arm ached powerfully in the evenings and was stiff and sore in the mornings. With God's help, he'd continue to heal and get closer to Nettie.

The lonely trail gave him time to think and plan for the future. He'd thought about his ranch a lot, but now his mind raced with how he could make it more appealing not only to Nettie, but also to Sam's wife and the few other women living in the surrounding area. The folks needed a church. He didn't know why he hadn't considered one before. They'd need a preacher too. Maybe he'd write to Billings and Great Falls to see if a preacher felt called to their area. If that didn't produce a man of God, then he'd search elsewhere. What a comforting thought to know the men would have something to do on Sunday mornings besides nurse bruises and hangovers from the night before, and the ladies could have their little meetings.

Riley smiled. Knowing his Nettie, she'd want to start up a temperance movement. A church sounded mighty fine, a place families could call their own. He and Nettie might contribute a real family. . .someday.

fifteen

Nettie hadn't heard a word from Montana. She knew the wire Maudie Mae had sent and the letter Nettie had mailed would take time, but she wanted to hear from Riley now. Where could he be? Had he changed his mind about wanting her with him?

Patience. She valued that virtue, and she practiced it well when she taught school because children needed compassion and understanding in order to learn and to respect others. This waiting to hear from her husband journeyed beyond patience; it involved love, fear, and a deep longing. And the idea of raising her baby without a father seemed more than she could bear.

As always when her thoughts assaulted her, Nettie prayed for Riley's safety and for God to work out the problems between them.

April eased into the first of May. Everywhere spring pushed through the soil with promise and hope. Maudie Mae urged her to move into town, but Nettie held out for a little longer, much to her friend's dismay. Maudie Mae, Celia, and Preacher Faulkner took turns visiting her, each one expressing their concern. In the meantime, Nettie grew bigger and more awkward. Some days she thought she'd burst like the colorful wildflowers decorating the plain—except that the flowers were pretty and delicate, and she didn't resemble anything close to their beauty.

The baby's new things sat in the soddie. One of the families from church donated a cradle, and the women from the temperance Bible class gave her a few more baby things. In one breath she felt ecstatic, and in the next she wept. Nettie knew emotions hit a woman with child hard, and she was no exception.

After Preacher Faulkner's call early one afternoon, Nettie took a nap. Her feet no longer looked like hers, and her body craved sleep. Simple chores had become a difficult undertaking, and the heavy work would have to wait. Taking care of a new baby could not be any worse than this. Toward dusk, she fetched the milk pail and made her way to the dugout.

Her home looked a little neglected—like it had before Riley arrived. Nettie had kept things neat and clean, but the fence needed repairs and the roof of the soddie appeared shabby. The judge had pressed her at church last Sunday about whether Riley intended to purchase the place.

"He's expected home any day now, Judge," Nettie said.

"Is he going to buy the land or not?"

"I'm not certain." Nettie didn't want to lie, but she didn't want to inform the judge of her departure until Riley joined her.

He pulled a handkerchief from his suit coat and wiped his brow. "Mighty warm for May. Please, Nettie, I need to know your decision soon. This isn't a charity case."

She sensed her face aflame. "The rent's been paid every month on time. I don't believe that constitutes a charity case."

"I'm thinking on selling that land. It's only fair to let me know what you're planning."

She felt a twinge of guilt. "I understand. I'll have word for you soon."

Now, as she bent over the cow and gasped for breath, she realized certain preparations must be made if Riley didn't return. She'd have to find a job and a place to live in Mesquite. Shaking her head, Nettie gave the matter over to the Lord. She'd take one day at a time.

Grabbing the milk pail handle, she headed toward the soddie. Warm milk and leftover corn bread from earlier in the day sounded tasty for supper, and she'd pour the rest of the milk into a jar for Celia and little Mary. Nettie had a hole behind the soddie in which she put milk, eggs, and butter to keep them cool. Some she gave to those in need, and the rest she sold to the boardinghouse. She placed the extra money into a cloth bag in a trunk under her bed.

Nettie climbed into bed, bone tired as usual. She said her prayers. Perhaps Riley would show up tomorrow. She had to think he would; she couldn't give up.

She awoke with a start and stared into the inky blackness. A sound from outside grasped her attention. Was it an animal, someone trying to steal her mule or the cow?

Nettie clumsily swung her legs over the side of the bed and pulled herself up. She had a rifle mounted over the front door, but her aim left a lot to be desired. At the very least, she could make some noise. Blinking to adjust her eyes to the darkness, she made her way to the door and lifted the rifle from its spot.

She heard the sound again, like someone going through things in the dugout. Slowly, she lifted the latch and tried to slip through the door, but her stomach got caught in the movement. Once outside, she raised the rifle. No point in firing into the dugout, she might kill the livestock.

"Get out of there." She pointed the rifle into the sky and squeezed the trigger.

"Nettie!"

She caught her breath. Had she heard right?

"Nettie! Don't fire. It's me."

She laid the rifle down, lifted her nightshirt above her ankles, and hurried toward the dugout.

❧

Riley heard Nettie calling his name long before she flew into his embrace. The moment she threw her arms around his neck, he knew something was different. She felt warm and smelled sweet just as he remembered, but she'd put on a little weight. No matter, being with his dear Nettie meant everything to him.

"My beautiful Nettie," he whispered, holding her as close as he could. "I've missed you every day I've been gone. I love you so much." Nettie laughed and cried at the same time, and he kissed her again and again.

"I've been worried sick."

"Aw, I'm sorry, Darlin'. I ran into a bit of trouble back in Montana. A grizzly didn't like me taking up room in his territory."

She gasped. "Are you all right?" She pulled back and touched both of his arms. "Here?" she asked, concentrating on the left side. "I can feel the bandage."

"It's healing fairly well. Won't be long before it's good as new. I really did get here as quickly as I could."

"Oh, Riley, I wish I could have helped with your nursing."

He smiled in the darkness. His dear Nettie, always ready to help out someone in need.

"Come on inside," she said. "Let me take a look at your wound and rustle up some food."

Arm in arm, they moved inside the soddie. Riley simply couldn't believe he'd finally arrived home. All those days laid up and dreaming about seeing her again. The first thing he wanted to do was light the lantern and stare into those gray eyes that haunted him night and day. He wanted to sit and gaze at her lovely face for hours.

"Is the lantern on the table?" he asked and trembled.

"Yes, I have it."

He swallowed hard while she struck a match and lit the wick. The light brightened the whole room, and then he saw her—really saw her.

His wife had not only added a few pounds; she was carrying his child.

"Nettie." What he'd meant as excitement came out as ragged words. "You. . .are you—"

She smiled, and all heaven could not have sparkled more than the love radiating from her face. "We're about to have a baby, Riley."

"I—I see." He couldn't keep his eyes from her bulging middle.

She reached for his hand. "The baby's jumping around in there, probably because he hears his papa's voice." She placed his rough hand overtop her stomach, and sure enough, Riley felt something move.

Startled, as though he'd touched a hot poker, he jerked back his hand.

Nettie laughed in a musical way. "Your child will not hurt you, Riley O'Connor." And she drew his hand back so he once more felt *his* baby move.

"Why didn't you tell me?" He drew her into his arms.

"I wanted it to be a surprise, and—"

He kissed the tip of her nose. "You're a stubborn one, Mrs. O'Connor."

"I'm sorry. I know how you feel about taking care of responsibilities, and I didn't want you coming back because of the baby. It's selfish, I know, but I wanted you coming back because you wanted me for your wife."

Riley nearly shed a few tears. "All I could think about over those long months was being with you. If I'd known you were carrying my baby, I'd have fought snowdrifts to get here sooner. You and me are what's important, Nettie, and I don't want us to ever be separated again."

"Me either." She nestled against his chest, just like he remembered.

"When can we expect him or her?" he asked, almost afraid to find out when.

"About a week or so." She toyed with a ragged edge of his coat collar. "We have a little while before our guest arrives."

Hours later, after they'd talked until Nettie fell asleep in his arms, he lay awake. *Lord, You've blessed me more than I deserve. Thank You for this baby, and I'm going to be needing You to show me how to be a proper father. And Lord, help my Nettie through this. My guess is she's a bit scared, this being her first baby. I know I am.*

How could he have been so stupid? His bullheadedness had caused him to miss the gradual change in his wife's small figure. His pride had told him a bunch of cows and horses in Montana meant more than the woman God intended for him to spend a lifetime with. The more he considered the reasons why he'd left Nettie, the more Riley realized what a fool he'd been.

Smiling into the darkness, he remembered Nettie saying she'd planned to bring the baby to Montana whether he came to Nebraska or not. She would have too. No doubt in his mind. He'd seen her resolute ways when the two were in jail.

Tomorrow he'd wire Sam to let him know about a delay in their return. He didn't want to set foot outside of Mesquite until the baby was born and Nettie felt up to a long trip. He wondered if the baby was a boy or girl. It didn't matter to him, just a healthy baby and mother. And names, what had she picked out?

I need to sleep. So much to do tomorrow. . . I want my child to have the best. Learn about God. Know how much his parents love him—or her.

❧

Nettie hadn't known such happiness since she and Riley first discovered how much they loved each other. All the pain of those days and weeks and months wishing he'd never left vanished the moment she heard his voice. This morning they'd slept late, still talking, laughing, and at times praying.

"Are you sure you want to visit Abe today?" Riley asked, breaking into her thoughts.

She touched his hand resting on her stomach. The baby had been kicking fiercely since Riley arrived. "He'll be so happy that you're home, and he's feeling poorly."

"Frank been to see him?"

"I don't think so. Celia and Mary call on Abe regular, though."

He released a heavy sigh. "I ought to try talking to Frank one more time."

She pressed a kiss to his auburn, whiskered jaw. "Maybe we'll learn he already has made his peace with Abe—and God."

A few hours later, Nettie and Riley arrived at Abe's. She remembered how he used to sit outside in warm weather, but this morning found him in bed. His pallor alarmed her, and his fever raged while the cough deepened in his chest. Abe looked too weak to fight off the death hounds at his door.

Nettie and Riley talked to him, one on each side of the failing old man.

"Glad yer home," Abe said, his raspy voice strained and labored. "Nettie needs you here with the baby."

"More like I need her," Riley said.

Abe offered a faint smile. "I felt that way about my wife. After all these years, I'm looking forward to seeing her again."

"I'd rather you stay close to us a little while longer." Nettie took his withered hand in hers.

"Naw. The Lord's calling me home." He let out a heavy sigh. "Sure do wish that son of mine would have come around. I'd like to tell Jesus that Frank made it. I'd like to think my son would spend eternity with me and his ma."

"I'm not giving up on him," Riley said. "Best I go fetch him today."

Nettie doubted if Abe could live through the week. Surely Frank would want to have a few parting words with his father. "Go on after him, Riley. I'll wait here."

Riley studied her closely. "The baby's not coming today?"

She tilted her head. How she adored his concern. "Not today. Go on now. Maybe you can catch him before he starts his evenin' drinking."

Riley hesitated until she confirmed again that he needed to find Frank without delay.

"I'll hurry." He picked up his hat on the table. "I'll stop by the judge's first. Don't want him throwing me in jail before I find Frank."

"He might help you," she said. "Either him or the sheriff."

Riley bent to offer her a kiss. "Promise me you won't do anything but sit here and talk to Abe."

She dampened her lips and a smile played on them. "No mending fences or chasing down cows?"

"Absolutely not."

"All right. I'll behave myself."

"Read to him from the Bible. When you're finished, why not talk about baby names or something?"

And right then, she knew exactly what to call her and Riley's baby. The thought made her giddy as a schoolgirl.

sixteen

Riley had a grim understanding of Abe's condition. The old man had hung on this long in hopes of his son accepting Jesus as his Savior, but the likelihood of Frank listening to Riley looked slim. If his wife couldn't persuade him, then how could Riley?

I can do all things. Remember, I delivered you.

Thank You, Lord.

Riley recalled how deep in sin he'd been before God had picked him up from the street and sent a messenger to minister words of hope and love. He wanted that for Frank and every other person who didn't know the Lord. This situation enforced Riley's desire to start a church in Montana. Too many cowboys and their families were without God. They needed a heavy dose of what Jesus wanted to do in their lives. Riley had a selfish reason too; he wanted his child raised around godly people.

Mesquite looked fairly deserted, and from the sun's position in the sky, Riley judged it was near noon. At the sheriff's office, he tied his mare to the hitching post and sauntered inside. Sheriff Kroft dozed in his chair, the snores rising like smoke signals, and his dime novel opened across his stomach.

"Sheriff Kroft," Riley said, wakening the man. "Can you tell me where I'd find Judge Balsh?"

The sheriff coughed and spurted. "What did you say?"

Riley wanted to laugh. "The judge. Where is he? It's about noon, I think."

"He's most likely at home."

After the sheriff gave directions, Riley moved on down the street to the other end of town. He admired the judge and

Maudie Mae's fine, wooden house. A porch wrapped around two sides, making it look real inviting. With a deep breath, Riley rapped on the door and waited for someone to answer.

"Afternoon, Riley," the judge said, stepping out onto the porch. "I've been expecting you."

Nettie had told him about the judge wanting to sell his land. "Afternoon." Riley removed his hat and stuck out his hand. "My call isn't about your land, but I do need to discuss another matter of importance."

Not a muscle moved on his face. "A serious matter?"

"Yes, Sir. Do you know Abe Wilkins?"

"Yes, I recollect I do."

"He's dying, Judge, and he's wanting to see his son, Frank." Riley shifted from one foot to the other. "I wondered if you'd help me persuade Frank to visit with Abe before it's too late."

The judge scratched his head. "Why me? Can't you do it yourself?"

"I could, but I might make Frank mad. My wife and I aren't his favorite people."

The big man nodded. "I understand. Let me tell Maudie Mae and get my hat. You're right, Riley. Frank isn't so likely to swing his fists and get rowdy if I'm with you."

At least this part had been easy. The two men readied their horses and rode out of town for about two miles to where Frank, Celia, and Mary lived. Celia worked at tilling up a garden, but Frank was nowhere in sight.

"Afternoon, Mrs. Wilkins," the judge said. "Is Frank around?"

She hesitated, then pointed to the soddie. "He's already drunk."

Riley saw the despair on the woman's face. How long would she allow herself and her daughter to be mistreated before she gave up?

"Let me talk to him first," the judge said as they dismounted. "He knows I don't have a problem throwing him in jail."

When Frank refused to answer the door, the judge hollered.

"This is Judge Balsh, Frank. Come on out so I can talk to you."

A string of cursing followed, but Frank managed to stumble out into the sunlight.

"I'm not wasting any time here. Your pa's dying and wants to see you," the judge said.

"I don't wanna see him," Frank said. "He's a stupid old man."

"No matter." Riley felt irritation gathering speed. "He's your father."

Frank squinted up at Riley. "Why are you here?"

"My wife is with your pa."

Frank chuckled. "Nettie? Now those two have plenty to talk about without me."

The judge cleared his throat. "You're going, Frank, or I'm taking you to jail for a good spell."

The man reeked of alcohol and sweat. The old smells haunted Riley worse than he cared to remember.

"I ain't done a thing to go to jail," Frank said.

"You're standing in the way of justice by refusing an old man's dying wish," the judge said.

Frank scowled, but in the end he swallowed down half a pot of strong coffee and mounted his mule. Without so much as a good-bye to his wife and daughter, he rode with the judge and Riley toward Abe's place. The combination of the hot brew and the spring sun appeared to sober Frank. His complaints lessened, and from Riley's guess, he was thinking on his pa.

Lord, I don't want to be putting notions into Your head, and I know this is between You and Frank. But I'm asking for some healing here between Abe and Frank.

Riley shot a glance at the judge. Maybe he wasn't such a bad fellow after all.

❧

Nettie waited and prayed for Frank to come before Abe breathed his last. She read Scripture and asked the old man about his favorite boyhood memories. Abe responded the best he could in between short naps.

Mid afternoon he took a turn for the worse. His words no longer made sense, and he talked to people who weren't there.

Hurry, Riley. There's little time left.

Nettie heard the men arrive and left Abe for only a moment. "Thank you for coming," she said to Frank. "He's nearly gone."

For the first time, emotion registered on Frank's face. He shook his head. "I can't go in there. I'm. . .I'm too ashamed of myself."

Nettie touched his arm. He looked awful and smelled even worse, but he was Abe's son, and the dear old man loved him. "Abe doesn't care what you've done; he loves you. Just come in and talk to him a little."

Frank closed his eyes. "All right." He looked over his shoulder at Riley. "Would you and your wife go with me? Riley, I reckon you're the only one here who knows what it's like to be a drunk."

Riley took Nettie's arm, and the three moved inside the soddie. She leaned over Abe's bed and whispered to him. "Abe, your son's here. Frank has come to see you."

Quite unexpectedly, the old man opened his eyes. Dark pools of blue, nearly black, cast love and warmth toward Frank. Abe held up his hand, and Frank awkwardly took it. Huge tears rolled over the old man's cheeks, and in the next instant, Frank sniffed.

"Glad you came, Son."

Frank swiped at his nose. "Are you hurtin'?"

"No, just tired, ready to meet Jesus and see your mother."

"Would you tell her I love her?"

Abe nodded. "I love you, Son. You're a fine man."

"I'm a drunk," Frank said, bitterness crusting his words. "Worthless, and I know it."

"God can change you."

"He don't want to hear from me."

Abe coughed, and Nettie feared he'd breathed his last. He hadn't spoken this much for several hours. Maybe he'd saved his strength.

"Yes. . .yes, He does. God's waiting for you."

"You were a good pa."

A faint smile graced Abe's lips. "Just try, Son. It's easy when you have a fine family like Celia and Mary." He breathed his last and his hand slipped from Frank's grasp. Frank laid his head on his pa's chest and sobbed. Nettie touched the grieving man's back, then reached for Riley. Frank needed to be alone.

Abe Wilkins was buried the following day in the cemetery behind Mesquite's church. Frank stayed sober and spoke kindly to everyone. So many people came forth with testimonies of the old man's kindness. He'd fed families, clothed children, and worked side-by-side with those who needed an extra hand in their fields. Nettie would never forget the Bible verse Preacher Faulkner used to describe Abe's life: "While we look not at the things which are seen, but at the things which are not seen; for the things which are seen are temporal; but the things which are not seen are eternal" (2 Corinthians 4:18).

The following Sunday, Frank attended church with Celia and Mary.

&

Riley observed his wife cooking fresh greens for dinner. They'd picked them together earlier in the day. Tired lines etched around her pretty gray eyes, and she moved slowly. As much as it scared him for his wife to give birth, it needed to happen soon. His dear Nettie looked miserable.

He stood from his chair. The reality of losing her in childbirth set hard on his mind. He didn't want to think of living without her. No amount of land in Montana or cows or horses could replace the woman he'd given his heart.

I'm giving her over to You, Lord. Take care of her and the baby.

Riley wrapped his arms around her ample waist and nuzzled his lips against her neck. "What can I do to help?"

She touched his cheek. "You can talk to me. I waited a long time to hear your voice, and I'll never tire of it again." Nettie peered up into his face. "What's wrong? You're fretting about something."

"Yes," he admitted. "I worry about you and the baby."

She shook her head. "I'm fine, healthy, and soon to be a mother."

"I know." The words came without much effort. "How long does it take for the baby to get here?"

"It depends. Since this is the first one, it may take awhile." She picked up a small sack of precious sugar. "I want to fix something special tonight."

He nodded. "A few hours?"

She sighed and reached for a pottery bowl. "Maybe a lot of hours."

Riley wished he hadn't been the youngest of six children. He knew nothing about birthing human babies—his experience was limited to animals giving birth. And something told him there was a difference. "Does it hurt the whole time?"

"No, the pains usually start out slow, then build up, getting closer together."

"And I can get the midwife in time?"

Nettie laughed. "We'll have plenty of time, Riley. Don't worry about a thing. Babies have been born since the beginning of time."

Not my baby.

She turned around and placed her hands on each side of his face. "I love you, Riley O'Connor, and your child will be here any day. Frettin' over it won't solve a thing."

He kissed her hands. "I've been praying about all this."

"Good. So let's talk about more pleasant things, like what do you want to call this baby?"

He shook his head. "Wish we knew if it was a boy or a girl."

Nettie found his words amusing and pulled him to a chair. She caught her breath. "Here are a few instructions from your wife. Don't worry about me. Don't worry about the baby. Don't worry about the midwife, and don't worry about if it's a boy or a girl. God will handle it all."

He kissed her soundly, but apprehension still pricked at his heart. Long after Nettie slept curled up next to him, Riley pondered the past several months. If he hadn't heeded God's Word, he'd be drunk this very minute with nothing to show for his life but empty bottles of whiskey. The way his life now looked reminded him of the passage in Romans that talked about how God took the bad and sinful things that happen to folks and used them for good.

Blessed best described Riley's world. He had a beautiful wife who loved him, his very own baby due any day, a piece of the most beautiful land on God's green earth, a Christian foreman, and the idea to start a church. What more could any man want?

Humility hit Riley hard. All of the things he cherished were nothing compared to the relationship he shared with Jesus Christ. If all his blessings vanished tomorrow, he'd still have the Lord. Riley smiled into the night. To some men, those thoughts might sound menacing, but he treasured the sound of them.

I'd like for you to start that church.

Riley felt certain he'd misunderstood.

I am, Lord. I'm going to scout around for the perfect spot to build Your house and run ads in some newspapers for a fittin' preacher.

Those people need a shepherd before the building's done or a minister is called to serve them.

Riley lay perfectly still. The thoughts running through his head must have come from his lack of sleep. He didn't know anything about preaching.

Follow Me, Riley.

He gulped. Did God want him to round up the folks at

home and start talking about His Word now? Before a real preacher arrived?

Yes. I will help you.

Riley closed his eyes. He saw a green piece of land in a valley on the far corner of his ranch. In the background he saw his beloved mountains reaching into the clouds. A gurgling stream wound around the back of the land, like one of Nettie's hair ribbons. A church painted in glistening white stood erect with a steeple and a cross. A towering oak tree sheltered the entrance, as though guarding anyone who came inside. On the steps, he saw Nettie wave. She held the hand of a child, but he couldn't tell if it was a boy or girl.

Nettie smiled and called to him. "Hurry, Riley. God's people need you."

Riley looked again and two boys called out, "Pa, we've been waiting."

Riley felt happiness nearly burst from his chest. He'd keep his secret until he and Nettie were on their way to Montana.

"Sweet Jesus," he said, barely above a whisper. "I will follow You all the days of my life."

seventeen

"Are you sure you feel well enough for church today?" Riley asked. His precious wife had deep circles under her huge eyes from tossing and turning all night. He'd given her his pillow to take some of the pressure off her back.

"Yes, I've been looking forward to it." She touched his chin with her finger. "Unless you think I waddle too much, and you don't want folks thinking you're married to a duck."

He chuckled and reached across the table to plant a kiss on her nose. They'd lingered over breakfast, talking about their new home in Montana—actually he'd done the talking, and Nettie had listened.

"If the fine folks of Mesquite think my wife looks like a duck, they haven't looked into her pretty face."

She blushed. "Oh, Riley, you always say I'm pretty, and right now I look like I'm ready to pop."

He leaned in closer and patted her stomach. "There is only one place where you are. . ."

She raised a brow, and he wrestled with the right words. Lately she cried at most everything, and he wanted to keep her smiling.

"A little bigger than normal, and that's where our baby is living," he said.

Her round face glistened with happiness. "I love you so much. I don't want to ever quarrel or fuss again. Let's be happy forever."

"Whatever you say." He gathered her hands into his and lifted her from the chair into his lap. Wrapping his arms around her middle, he held her close. Riley knew there would be many times in the future when disagreements would come between them, but that came with growing together and getting to know each other. Snuggling against her neck, he stifled a chuckle. This sweet woman on his lap could flare up at a moment's notice, but right now she reminded him of a little bitty girl.

❧

Preacher Faulkner's sermon that morning pierced Nettie's heart. He spoke about wives submitting to their husbands and husbands loving their wives as Christ loved the church. She knew if she'd been obedient to God last September, she wouldn't have spent all those months alone without Riley. Granted, they were both bullheaded about many things, down right stubborn at times, but they did love God and each other. When she considered how she nearly lost Riley to a grizzly, she shuddered. Riley's arm was healing fine, although he'd carry some nasty scars.

Scars. Riley carried the mark along his face that ushered him to God, and he bore the marks on his arm that brought him back to her. Strange how things happened, but Nettie didn't believe in coincidence. She maintained God's hand rested in every aspect of a person's life. When she thought back over her past, she could see Him putting people and circumstances in her life to make her stronger.

Nettie and Riley visited with friends after church. Maudie Mae invited them to dinner, but Nettie knew she'd have a difficult time staying awake. In addition, she didn't want Riley to sit through the judge wanting to know if they intended to purchase his land.

"I'd love to come to dinner, but I'm exhausted. Perhaps another time?" Nettie asked.

"Most certainly," Maudie Mae said. "You do look tired."

"I'll get the wagon," Riley said. "Go ahead and talk with Maudie Mae while I bring it around." The judge followed Riley, no doubt wanting to discuss business.

"He's a good man," Maudie Mae said once Riley stepped

beyond hearing distance. "And he dearly loves you."

Nettie's toes tingled. "Yes, he is far more than I ever deserved."

"Have you decided where you'll live?" Maudie Mae asked. "I'm not asking for the judge; I simply don't want to lose our friendship."

Nettie glanced away. Lying didn't rest well with her, especially on Sundays in the churchyard.

"Never mind," Maudie Mae said. "I'm sure you and Riley know what is best for your family." She patted her pocket. "Forgive me, Nettie, I nearly forgot this. Yesterday I stopped at the telegraph office, and a message came through for Riley." Handing her the telegram, Maudie Mae peered over her shoulder. "Aren't you going to read it? I wouldn't be able to contain myself."

Nettie looked at the folded piece of paper.

"I know what you're thinking, and I didn't." Maudie Mae crossed her arms and slid a glance at Nettie. "But I really wanted to. I did find out it's from Montana."

Nettie shook her head and giggled. She turned the telegram over in her hands. "I'm sure Riley will tell me the contents, and I thank you for delivering it."

"Riley will contact me about the baby? I can assist the midwife."

From experience, Nettie knew the midwife didn't need additional help. Most times folks simply got in the way. "We'll keep you informed," Nettie said. "I don't think it will be long."

Riley waved and headed her way. She gave Maudie Mae a quick hug, the best she could do in her current physical condition, and said good-bye.

"I have something for you," Nettie said once they pulled away from the church and had headed out of town. "Maudie Mae picked up a telegram for you."

"Must be news from Sam. Why don't you read it to me, Honey?"

The sun beat down warm, a little too warm for Nettie. Heat never affected her in the spring, but she hadn't been nine months with child before either. She fanned herself with her hand, then carefully opened the piece of paper. Clearing her throat and sitting straighter on the wagon seat, she began to read.

" 'Riley, the Watering Hole is doing good. Many of your ladies have little ones.' "

Nettie dropped the telegram on her lap. Immediately her stomach fluttered, and she squeezed her hands to stop the shaking. This couldn't be happening. She moistened her dry lips while the truth marched across her mind: Riley had lied to her.

"What's wrong?" Riley asked. "You're pale. Is it the baby? Do we need to turn around and head back to town? What can I do?"

She grasped the paper in her fingers, her stomach churning. "The Watering Hole? What does this mean?" Nettie swallowed hard. "Your little ladies giving birth? How do you explain that, Riley?"

Riley leaned his head back and laughed until he clutched his sides. The sound echoed about the countryside, but Nettie failed to find anything amusing about the words.

"What is so funny?" she asked.

"You," he said. "Shall I interpret Sam's message for you?"

Nettie gritted her teeth. "I think I understand perfectly."

Riley's demeanor changed. "Why, you're serious, Nettie. This is nothing. The Watering Hole is the name of my ranch, and the ladies are the cows. We were expecting a large number of calves this spring, and looks like we got 'em."

The odd sensation piercing her heart refused to give way. Whoever heard of a ranch called the Watering Hole? That was the name of a saloon—and cows were not called ladies. What had he been doing in Montana?

"You lied to me, Riley O'Connor. You lied to me about everything."

❧

Riley refused to believe his ears. What had been funny hadn't affected his wife in the same way. Nettie didn't make sense, and what did she mean by him lying to her? Bewildered, he wondered how a simple telegram could rile a woman into such a fit of anger. Dazed by the sudden turn of her mood, he looked at her with his mouth agape.

"Honey—"

"Don't you dare 'honey' me. You led me to believe you had a ranch in Montana, and now I see your business is a saloon!"

"A saloon? Calm down, Nettie. You know I gave up drinking when I found the Lord." The accusation made him a bit agitated, and the more her accusation settled in his mind, the angrier he grew.

She lifted her chin and glared at him like a rattler ready to strike. "Are you using the Lord as an excuse to drink or entice other poor men to sell their souls to whiskey?"

"You've gone far enough. I've explained Sam's telegram to the best of my ability, and I don't know what else you want from me. You've called me a liar and questioned my salvation." His words were spoken as savagely as he felt, and Riley had no intention of backing down. She'd made him mad, really mad.

"When it comes to drinking and collaborating with those who do, I don't trust anyone." Her lips quivered, and he waited for the onslaught of tears.

Riley pulled the mule to a halt and leaned an elbow on one knee while he watched his wife. "I know you don't feel good right now, and I forgive your hurtful words, but frankly Nettie, you stabbed me pretty good. I love you, and I've never lied to you about anything."

Lightning flashed across her gray eyes. She turned her

attention to the road. Nettie neither uttered a word nor looked at him the rest of the way home.

Lord, how do I remedy this? Is the problem 'cause she's about to have a baby? If so, I don't think we're having any more.

⋰

While Riley unhitched the wagon, Nettie left him alone and made her way to the soddie. Her back ached, she felt dizzy, but even worse, a knife twisted in her heart.

The telegram's message repeated in her mind. No matter how hard she tried to erase the awful words, they stabbed her soul. The man she loved, her husband, had lied. Fury swelled inside her. The coward didn't have enough backbone to own up to the truth once she held it in her hands.

The Watering Hole. Although the thought made her ill and she despised the implication, still an image of Riley leaning over a bar stayed fixed in her mind. She imagined him ordering whiskey for everyone in the place and laughing with *those* kind of women.

Had Riley been unfaithful? Dare she even blame him? After all, her words had driven him away. Tears streamed down Nettie's face, and she no longer tried to stop them. Burying her face in her hands, all she could think about was how she'd been wronged by the man she loved—the father of her unborn child.

Alcohol, the root of evil, Satan's brew. It had its fingers in Riley and refused to let him go. But she knew the nightmare of living in a family with a man consumed by whiskey's fire, and she dare not do the same for her baby. Love never cured a drunk, it merely gave him an excuse to drink more. She'd seen it enough to accept the reality. Better she raised her baby alone than risk the same life with Riley.

"Talk to me, Honey."

Nettie lifted her face to see him. This must be the last time. She'd memorize every inch of his rugged features and seal them in her heart. If the consequences were only hers to bear, she'd risk it. But her desires were selfish, and she had more to consider than her own feelings.

"I don't know what else to say," Riley said, moving toward her. "I spoke the truth. Do you want to wire Sam and ask him your questions? I could send another telegram in the morning."

"No, I couldn't bear it." Nettie rose from the chair, her body awkward and weary. She gripped the wooden back for support. "I won't be made a fool, like my. . ." Shaking her head, she found the courage to take her stand.

"Please, Honey. Rest for awhile. When you get up, we can talk about this." Riley looked earnest, as though she had been mistaken. "Let me help you to bed."

She'd heard all the clever excuses for drinking and all the empty promises of leaving it alone. She'd witnessed what happened when it took over a man's body and soul. Covering her ears, she remembered doing the same thing when her father returned home and said all the right things to her mother. Nettie wanted to scream and tell her father to go away. He spoke lies, and her mother believed him. For a few days, home became a place of pretended love and laughter, then he'd slip out and come home hours later—drunk and mean.

"No," Nettie cried and hurried toward the bedroom. "Leave me alone. I can't ever trust you again. I refuse to be that stupid."

Riley grabbed her arm. Confusion stared back at her. "I don't understand your reaction to this. You've gotten yourself all worked up over nothing."

"Nothing?" she questioned over her shoulder. "I guess you would say that."

eighteen

Nettie asked Riley to sleep next to the fireplace that night. She couldn't bear to have him near her. The scent of him, his touch, and the sound of his even breathing had become a vital part of her existence. Tears no longer graced her eyes, but in their place towered a fierce determination to establish a life for herself and her baby.

Strange, her husband shed no emotion at her request. He simply took the quilt and pillow she offered and bedded down on the floor.

After a sleepless night, she awoke before dawn and dressed in the only dress that fit her—a borrowed one from Celia. Making her way into the other room, Nettie expected to see Riley, but he'd gone. Nothing remained but a folded quilt.

He's gotten up early to milk. When Nettie opened the door and peered at the dugout, she saw neither her husband nor the lantern. Curiosity nibbled at her mind. Where could he have gone? She lit the candle on the table and took it with her to the dugout.

Riley's chestnut mare was gone. Nettie realized he must have left for good. She'd been right all along. Using the back of the dugout as a brace, she leaned back and closed her eyes.

Father, thank You for opening my eyes. I nearly made another terrible mistake. Be with Riley. I do love him dearly. Help him to understand the evils of strong drink and how it will eventually kill him.

With her heart broken over a man who had betrayed her, she headed back toward the soddie. The baby would be coming any day. She needed to be in Mesquite where the midwife could help her. Praise God she'd hidden money away in the trunk beneath her bed. She'd be fine. As long as she continued to reassure herself of that fact, she'd take one minute at a time.

All the plans she and Riley had made were nothing more than childish dreams. They'd meant nothing to him. Did he think she wouldn't have turned around and trekked back to Nebraska once she learned he didn't own a ranch? She loved Riley so much. They could have shared a fine life together.

Nettie put together a few things for her and the baby, then hitched up the mule to the wagon. As the sun brightened up the early morning sky and fingers of light touched the ground, she urged the mule west toward Mesquite. When the baby came, she'd no longer feel depressed. She'd have the joy of a new birth to take away the agony of losing Riley. God would be her husband and a Father to her child. Children were intended to have both earthly parents, but God had a special plan for this one.

Once in Mesquite, Nettie found a room at the boarding-house. The owner carried her belongings to the room and offered to take her wagon and mule to the livery. The man was indeed a blessing. Although Nettie's quarters were small, Hilda kept the area clean and tidy. A faint smile swept through Nettie. Maybe she could give the woman cooking lessons. Maybe if she were good enough, the boardinghouse might hire her on as a cook. That way she and the baby would have a place to live too.

After placing her few things in the drawers, she ventured downstairs and out into the day. The first item on her agenda came with a visit to the midwife, informing her of Nettie's temporary living arrangements at the boardinghouse. Afterward she planned to visit Maudie Mae. By then exhaustion would overcome her, and she'd be sleeping the rest of the afternoon.

Sitting on Maudie Mae's velvet green sofa and sipping tea

from delicate porcelain cups hadn't made Nettie feel any better about her circumstances.

"And Riley's gone?" Maudie Mae frowned. "Without a word?"

Nettie nodded. "No note or anything. I've been deceived, and it hurts terribly."

Her friend rested her cup on the parlor table. "Could you have been wrong? Perhaps the ranch is called the Watering Hole, and it saw new calves this spring."

"Why didn't Sam say as much in the telegram? I wish I were wrong, but the past stares me in the face." Nettie wanted to lean back against the sofa, but a proper lady always possessed excellent posture.

"Nettie," said Maudie Mae in her high-pitched voice. "You look so very tired. Why don't you rest here? No one will bother you."

She attempted a half smile. "You're right. I am ready to fall asleep. I appreciate your generosity, but I think I'll walk back to the boardinghouse."

"Would you like for me to have the horse and wagon hitched up?"

"Nonsense," Nettie said. "I'm fine. And I do appreciate you listening to my problems." She bid her friend good-bye and slowly made her way to the boardinghouse. After she rested, the future promised to look brighter.

❧

Riley returned from a ride to Abe's old place. The old man had been the first to give him a word from the Lord, and Riley wanted to think the land held a spark of holiness. His first ride from Montana to Mesquite centered on finding Abe and returning the Bible. Times afterwards, he had visited the old man with the idea of assisting him in some way, but Riley always received the most. In any event, that's where he rode in the predawn hours seeking the Lord. The situation between him and Nettie must be resolved and soon. For the life of him, he couldn't figure out where she got those outlandish ideas. Sure, Sam worded the telegram strangely, but Nettie should have taken Riley's word about the matter.

Deliberating over the matter didn't give him direction about his wife and their future. He must make her see he'd spoken the truth.

Riding in sight of the soddie he shared with Nettie, Riley sensed a peace come over him. Prayer had certainly helped, and he felt the Lord riding right beside him. After a good night's sleep, Nettie must remember how much they loved each other. Troubles were bound to come, but they had to talk things out instead of fussin'.

As soon as he pulled in next to the dugout, Riley saw she'd taken the wagon and mule. She must be gone to Mesquite. This time, she'd left him. His stomach growled, but no matter, he intended to ride into town and fetch his wife. What would she do if the baby decided to come?

All the way to Mesquite, Riley's anger mounted. A woman in her condition had no business going out alone. What if the baby decided to come while on the road? She'd be alone and. . .well, Riley refused to think about the outcome.

Just as he suspected, the mule and wagon were at the livery.

"I have no idea how long your wife intended to leave them," the livery attendant said. "Roy left them here."

Riley willed himself not to say anything about Nettie's foolishness. Instead he thanked him and headed to the boarding-house. His prior visit to the establishment had given him a horrible headache and a stay in jail. He hoped this trip had more to offer, although he wasn't looking to it in the way of food. Riley had sensed hunger pains for a long time, but they weren't bad enough to make him willing to eat rock-hard corn bread.

"G'morning," Riley said to Roy.

The man recognized him immediately. "What can I do for you, Riley?"

"I believe my wife is staying here. Her name's Nettie O'Connor."

The man lifted a brow. "Uh, yes, she checked in this morning."

"I'd like to talk to her. What room is she in?"

The man cleared his throat, then scratched his head. "She didn't want me telling you what room, but since I owe you for the time you did in jail, I'll help you out." He pointed up the stairs. "It's the second room on the right. She looked plum tuckered out when she came in a little bit ago."

Riley gave him a grim smile and took the stairs two at a time. Standing in front of the designated door, he took a deep breath before knocking. "Nettie, this is me, Riley. We need to talk, Honey. Open the door."

Silence.

He tapped his boot on the wooden floor and waited.

Silence.

"Nettie, I'm asking you real sweet-like to open the door. We need to talk about this before the baby gets here." How could one woman be so stubborn? Worse yet, how could he love a woman so much when she made him so downright angry?

Silence.

Riley stood there for several long moments more. "All right, Honey. If you don't want to talk, I'll go see Maudie Mae. I'm sure she can explain all of this to me." He stomped down the steps, out the door, and down the street. A dog chased him part of the way, which didn't help his mood at all.

With his hat in hand, Riley knocked on the Balshes' door. He considered what he'd say and do if Maudie Mae slammed the door in his face, but until that happened, he'd remain calm and reasonable.

"Yes, Riley." She smiled broadly, but the gesture didn't fool him at all.

"Maudie Mae, you and I both know my wife is at the boardinghouse. She won't open the door, and for the life of me, I can't figure out why she's so riled she left me."

Maudie Mae lifted her chin and pressed her palms together. "Nettie told me everything, and I am quite appalled at your behavior."

He wanted to slam his fist into the side of the house. "What behavior? I received a telegram from my foreman stating the ranch is fine and the cows have given us calves. She's been upset ever since."

Maudie Mae eyed him down her long nose. "Riley, are you telling me the truth?"

"I'd swear on God's Word. We planned to head to Montana as soon as she and the baby could handle the trip."

She hesitated. "How much do you know about your wife's family?"

He shrugged. "She hasn't said much. I know she didn't marry young because of tending to sick parents."

"Anything else?"

Frustrated best termed Riley's feelings. Why couldn't women just state what was on their minds and be done with it? "No, nothing, but what are you not telling me?"

Maudie Mae eyed him a moment more before opening the door and inviting him inside. She pointed to the dimly lit parlor and proceeded to light a lantern. "Sit down, Riley. I think it's time you learned a few things about your wife."

He wondered how a man was supposed to sit on such a fancy chair and hoped he didn't touch anything valuable. Irritating the judge didn't rest well with him.

"What can I get for you?" Maudie Mae asked. "Coffee, something to eat?"

"Nothing, thank you. I really want to understand my wife, if you don't mind."

She nodded and began. "Nettie's involvement with the

temperance movement didn't begin here in Mesquite. She's been active in the organization for several years, and there's a reason for it."

Riley leaned in closer so as not to miss a word. Maudie Mae and Nettie were friends and most likely shared all sorts of women talk. He hoped someday Nettie would share her heart with him.

A matter plagued him. How long had Maudie Mae endured the judge owning a saloon while he sat in the front pew each Sunday? In that instant, he pitied Maudie Mae. Riley imagined a wealth of wisdom rested in her heart.

"Nettie's father had a drinking problem," she began. "I guess the best comparison is Frank Wilkins before he got right with the Lord. Nettie's father came home drunk and mean almost every night. He'd beat her mother until the poor woman couldn't move. Nettie watched all of it. He never laid a hand on his daughter, but the fear stayed with her nevertheless. Nettie tended to her mother and helped as much as she could."

Now he understood her aversion to whiskey and her unusual responses to anything resembling alcohol.

"The beatings eventually sent Nettie's mother to bed. Nettie doctored her the best she could, but the woman's body had been hurt too many times. Not long afterward, her father took to bed from all the drinking he'd done. Nettie had both parents to nurse and support. That's when she learned about being a midwife. Fortunately while her father lay bedridden, he realized the damage he'd done to his family. He called on the Lord to save him and went to his grave a Christian. Nettie's mother died soon afterward."

"That's why she acts suspicious of everything I say and do," Riley said. "She's afraid I'm not really a believer and worries I'm drinking behind her back."

Maudie Mae nodded. "I don't doubt you told her the truth.

I can see how much you love her, and I see your commitment to Jesus in your eyes. Right now she's scared about delivering this baby and worried she's going to turn out like her mother."

Riley needed a moment to collect his thoughts. The happenings in Nettie's life made her reactions to things as clear as a mountain stream. "Thank you for telling me all this. I guess only God can heal her heart and let her see how much I care."

Maudie Mae laid her hand across his. "I'll be praying for both of you."

Riley left the house feeling a heavy burden that only God could lift. What Maudie Mae had told him explained Nettie's behavior, but he had no idea how to make her see the truth. When he considered her as a little girl watching her father's drunkenness destroy her mother, his heart went out to Nettie. Everything now made sense. How sad for her parents to die prematurely when it all could have been prevented. As Riley walked, he pondered the situation. Somehow he ended up at the parsonage.

"You look like a troubled man," Preacher Faulkner said. His round cheeks were tinged pink from pulling weeds around his home. He looked different without his black, wide-brimmed hat and preacher's collar. "Come sit a spell on my porch. We can talk."

"I could use some advice." Riley shook the preacher's hand and took a seat on the porch steps. "It's about Nettie and me. . . ."

"She's carrying a load that should have been given to God," Preacher Faulkner said once Riley finished. "Your wife has such a kind spirit. Most anyone else would be bitter. I remember when I suggested she give aid to those at the saloon, and she wasted no time doing that very thing."

Riley stretched his long legs. "How can we help her? I want my wife to love me and trust that I will always do my best to follow the Lord."

A dog trotted up to the preacher's side. The animal wagged

its tail, but when Preacher Faulkner reached to pet its head, the dog growled and backed away.

"Some folks are like this stray dog, Riley. They crave love and affection, but when it's offered, they back off. I don't mean to be comparing your dear wife to a dog, but the same principle holds true. She wants your devotion, but she's afraid of being hurt. I bet if I took the time to feed this dog and speak kindly, one day it would stand still and enjoy my attention."

Riley understood, but he didn't have time to wait on Nettie forever. They were about to have a baby. As though reading his mind, the preacher continued.

"You've loved and taken care of Nettie, and you proved it by returning to Mesquite. But sometimes she's still afraid and runs. This is one of those times."

"What do I do? I don't want to make anymore mistakes." He buried his face in his hands. "I've failed God and my wife."

"You haven't failed Him, and He knows your heart."

Riley lifted his head and met Preacher Faulkner's gaze. "I'm willing to sell my ranch and stay here in Nebraska if that's what it'll take to keep Nettie."

"We need to pray for God's guidance. I suggest you go back to the boardinghouse and tell her your heart. And you keep coming back with the same message until she understands you're not about to leave her or forsake her."

nineteen

Riley entered the boardinghouse with renewed energy to win his wife's trust. Roy greeted him with an offer of a free meal.

"Hilda's doing a little better with her cooking, but I made a pot of ham and beans if you're interested. Got fresh corn bread too."

Riley hadn't eaten all day, but he had a mission. Glancing up the stairs, he realized Nettie must come first. "Let me pay you for tonight, because I intend to camp outside Nettie's door. I'm powerful hungry too. Can I eat upstairs?"

Roy nodded. "You must love that wife of yours a heap."

"I do." Riley pulled out his money. "Is her room paid?" When Roy replied affirmatively, he slapped a few bills on the counter. "Here's a little extra to bring the food up to me."

Roy motioned to Nettie's room. "Hilda took supper up to her about an hour ago, so I know she's there."

Riley headed up the stairs again and knocked, not that he expected Nettie to answer. "Honey, I'm right here, and I'm not leaving. I'm staying as close to you as I can until you're ready to talk."

The silence tore at his heart.

"Honey, I talked to Maudie Mae." He lowered his voice, knowing Roy and Hilda were within earshot. "I know about your papa, all the things he did to your mama and you. I understand you're afraid to really trust me, but I swear to you I haven't had a drop of whiskey since Abe pulled me from the street almost five years ago." He paused, hoping for a response. "My ranch in Montana is the Watering Hole. I named it when I saw all the lakes and streams on the land.

Sam's always called the cows ladies; it's just his way."

Still she did not respond.

"Honey, I'll sell my ranch and stay here in Nebraska if that's what you want. I can buy the judge's land and learn farmin'. I love you, and I'll do whatever you want to keep us together. God put us together, Nettie, and I won't let anything separate us again."

When silence met his ears, he tried one last time.

"Honey, I'm not your papa and I never will be. I don't make promises I can't keep. All I'm askin' is another chance." Riley sat on the floor and looked at the dinner Roy had brought him. It smelled good, but he didn't feel like eating.

God held his life with Nettie in the palm of His hand.

❧

Nettie had listened to Riley's every word while she lay on the bed. She sensed an urging in her spirit to open the door and tell him of all the love in her heart. But fear paralyzed her body. He could very well be deceiving her, filling her with empty promises.

When Riley told her he knew about her father, she nearly cried out. Without warning, the memories crept over her like a dark shroud. The times she hid. The times she felt ashamed because she did nothing while he beat her mother. The mass of bruises on her mother's face. Later would come her father's promises and apologies. Those remembrances were what hurt Nettie the most.

Riley is not your father. He's a man of God.

She gasped. The inner voice reminded her of a calm breeze on a summer day—refreshing, gentle. She wanted to reach out and touch the feeling it offered to her soul.

I'm afraid, Lord. I don't want my baby to face the nightmares I did.
Trust me, Daughter.

Nettie let the words settle in her mind. Trust. Every relationship involved this freedom from doubt and despair. To her, it meant a belief in a person's character. She wanted to grasp those qualities with Riley, but she couldn't do it alone.

Take My hand. Let Me lead you through the valley.

Tears slipped from Nettie's eyes. *Forgive me, Lord. I pray it's not too late with my husband.*

She moved clumsily to the side of the bed and managed to swing her legs to the floor. A candle on the dresser caught her attention, and she rose to light it. When the shadows danced on the walls, she allowed her gaze to sweep around the small room. This wasn't home, not if she kept Riley locked outside her life. Neither the finest house nor the biggest city could ever be home if Riley didn't walk beside her. He wanted to build their future in Montana, and she belonged there too.

Nettie smoothed her hair and the wrinkled dress covering her bulging body. She stepped to the door and quietly unlocked it.

And it happened.

Her water broke, soaking her clothes and the floor. Mortified, she refused to allow Riley to see her this way. She didn't have another dress. How could she summon the midwife? Hilda would gladly go for her, but getting her attention meant exposing her wet clothes. Nettie did her best to mop up the floor with a towel placed by the washbasin. She started to straighten, and a stab of pain shot through her abdomen. Biting on her lip, she waited for the sensation to pass before she moved again.

Nettie reached for the bed and curled on top of it. Riley, she needed him to help her, but she looked unsightly. Another pain caused her to hold her breath. These were too close together for her liking. She needed time to prepare. Horror swept over her; she hadn't brought any herbs. In her haste to leave Riley, she'd merely concerned herself with clothes—nothing to help through the birthing. The midwife carried those things, so Nettie had put the matter out of her mind.

Another pain soared through her, lasting longer, deeper in its intensity. The baby had no thoughts of a lengthy labor.

She remembered a few babies who came quickly, but most took hours of work, especially the first ones.

I'll wait awhile and rest. I have plenty of time.

For the next two hours, Nettie rested fitfully. Between pains, she listened for Riley. Perhaps he'd given up and not stayed by the door. How could she blame him? She must get help.

"Riley." She attempted to sound strong. "Riley, can you hear me?"

"Yes."

"I'm terribly sorry for everything." She held her breath as the baby pressed hard against her.

"It's all right, Honey. We can talk this out."

She waited until the pain subsided. "I wanted to look pretty when I saw you again, but something's happened."

"What?" His voice edged with alarm. She must not have hidden her agony.

"The baby's coming—much faster than I thought. I need you, Riley. Please come in. The door's—" She bit down on her lip and squeezed her eyes shut.

The door opened. "Nettie! Oh my! What can I do? Why didn't you tell me?"

She opened her eyes and stared into the face of her beloved husband. "I was embarrassed. I look awful."

He bent over the bed and kissed the tip of her nose. "You are the most beautiful woman in the whole world."

"I love you," she said.

He took her hand, and in the next instant, another pain wracked her body. She squeezed his hand until the time passed.

"I'd better get the midwife." Perspiration dripped from the sides of Riley's face.

Nettie shook her head. "Don't leave me, please."

"All right. I'll holler for Roy or Hilda to fetch her." He glanced at her hand clinging to his. "Honey, you'll have to let go of me."

Nettie released her grip. She watched him take two long strides to the door. "Roy, Hilda. Nettie's havin' the baby. Would you fetch the midwife?" As soon as he heard an answer, he hurried back to her.

The pains attacked her a minute apart, each one seeming to tear her body in half. She refused to cry out, only grip Riley's hand harder. Clamping down on her lip, tasting the blood, she stared into his face.

"Honey, scream or do something if you will feel better."

She couldn't frighten him anymore than he already was if the lines on his face were any indication.

"Where is the midwife?" The frustration in his voice echoed his concern.

Babies weren't supposed to arrive with fathers standing by helplessly. He needed to be waiting somewhere—drinking coffee and letting her do the work. She hated the frightened look on his face.

Nettie dragged her tongue over parched lips. "It's too late. The baby's coming now."

He paled. "What am I supposed to do?"

"Wash your hands." She swallowed hard and breathed a prayer. "I'll talk you through this."

"Where's the towel?" Riley asked, watching her as he did her bidding. "What kind of a boardinghouse is this?

Before she could reply, the pains sharpened, and instantly Riley stood at her side, his hands dripping.

"This can't be much different than birthing a cow or a horse," he said, but disbelief laced his voice.

Several seconds later she finally replied. " 'Tisn't much difference. Best be ready."

&

Riley shivered. In his arms slept a baby boy, his son. "He's perfect. Look at him, Honey. I've never seen anything so beautiful in all my life, 'cept his mother."

He laid the baby next to Nettie and saw the love shimmer from her eyes. "Oh, Riley, we did this. You, me, and God. I've seen so many new babies, but none as fine as ours."

"What do you want to name him?"

She glanced up and saw the pride written in Riley's eyes. "He looks like an Abraham Riley O'Connor to me."

Another pain coursed through her body. Nettie trembled. Had something gone wrong? "Riley, I think there's another baby."

A moment later, Riley held another son. This time the tears flowed unchecked. His vision of what God promised settled in his mind. "Look at them, Honey. We've been blessed with two." He lay the second baby on her other side.

She examined every inch of the second babe, just as she had Abraham. Riley observed her every move. This woman he loved so dearly had given him two precious sons. What more could any man ever want? She lifted her gaze to him. "What do we call this one?"

Riley felt his heart swelling as though it might burst. "I don't know for sure. I've always been partial to Aaron."

Her raven hair glistened wet against the pillow. "That's a fine name. What could we put with it?"

He rubbed his chin. "What is Preacher Faulkner's given name?"

She tilted her head a bit. "James."

"Aaron James O'Connor sounds like a good name to me."

"Perfect," she said. Exhaustion seemed to overtake her.

A knock at the door and Hilda's insistent voice captured their attention. The midwife had arrived.

"We have twins," Riley said, standing his full height.

"I'm Mary." The white-haired woman grinned at the infants. "Looks like congratulations are in order."

"Thank you, Ma'am."

She linked her arm into Riley's and walked him toward the hall. "And I have work to do. Shoo on out of here, Papa.

Hilda, you could draw some water so these boys can get cleaned up."

Hilda bustled by Riley and down the stairs. He heard Mary speak kindly to his Nettie. The ah's danced around his ears like sweet angel's music. For the next several moments, he basked in his sons' glorious births. He rolled their names around on his tongue and imagined all the things they'd be doing one day—first words, first steps, puppies, ponies, frogs, and fishin'. What a grand time they'd have, and what a wonderful mama too. Life couldn't be better. God had a way of blessing a man no matter how bad he'd once been.

The minutes ticked by, and he heard nothing. Impatience picked at him. He wanted to see his wife and his sons. Thirty minutes passed before Mary opened the door. A grim look creased her face and it scared him.

"Mr. O'Connor, would you step in please?"

Riley trembled. "Are the babies all right? What's wrong?"

One glimpse of Nettie told it all. She'd turned a ghastly shade of white, and the babies had taken residence in dresser drawers.

"She's lost a lot of blood," Mary said. "I've done all I can do. You might want to have a word with her."

The truth lay in what Mary failed to say. Final words? Was his dear Nettie about to die? *Oh, no, God. This can't be in Your plan.* "Have you been praying?" he asked a bit harshly.

"Yes, we have."

But I haven't. Devastated, yet refusing to accept Mary's words, Riley took Nettie's hand and dropped to his knees. She smiled faintly and closed her eyes.

"Pray for me," she said through a shallow breath. "But promise me this."

"Yes, Honey, whatever you want."

"Take. . .take our sons to Montana."

"You're goin' too." He wanted to cry; even more, he wanted to scream the unfairness of it all. "Let me pray. God has answered our prayers before, and I have faith He will again."

Riley choked back the sobs. How could such joy bring such sadness? "Heavenly Father, You know I'm scared about Nettie, but I know You can make her strong again. I beg of You to touch her with Your healing power. I don't mean to be a selfish man, but I need her, Lord. I want to spend the rest of my life taking care of her and my sons. I ask You to not take Nettie from me and those who love her, amen."

He looked into the face of his sweet wife. His stomach bubbled and twisted. Every part of him ached for her. *Why can't I be the one near death? Oh, Lord, I'd gladly change places.*

"Thank you." Nettie spoke through closed eyes. "I love you; I'll always love you."

Mary laid her hand on his shoulder. "Hilda and I will wait downstairs. She is in God's hands. I don't want to build false hopes, but. . .she's very ill."

"I'm expecting a miracle." Riley caressed Nettie's cheek "Someday we'll tell our sons how God stopped the angels of death."

Alone with his wife, Riley wept and prayed. Fear yanked at his being, as though mocking him for every moment he had not lived for the Lord. He remembered every cross word and those moments when he could have responded in love instead of running. His feelings didn't come from God, but they assaulted him nevertheless. He stole a glimpse at his sons. No sound came from the tiny babes, as though they knew their mother bordered between life and death. Without Nettie, he'd raise their sons alone. He could, with the help of God, but babies needed their mother. He needed her. The thought of staring into the eyes of those boys and always catching a sweet remembrance of Nettie moved him to swipe away the tears.

Studying the ashen face of his beloved and hearing her labored breathing brought him to the floor, prostrate to the only One who could heal her.

twenty

Nettie dreamed of floating among the clouds. She felt weightless and serenely happy. The pain she'd endured during and after the birth of her sons vanished the moment she'd given in to blissful sleep. Extending her arms to touch the fluffy, white billows, she allowed them to gently caress her entire body. Nettie recalled snowflakes lighting on her face and mouth. Their beauty matched no other but was still incomparable to these clouds.

What a glorious sensation, a bit of heaven for her to treasure until the day she met Jesus face to face. This feeling could only be compared to resting in the palm of His hand.

A scent of flowers, not exactly tender blossoms but a delicate aroma that invoked memories of love and joy, swirled about her. Perhaps the clouds held the enticing smells. She wasn't sure, and her heart had filled so much with peace that she didn't care to deliberate on the matter.

A taste of sweetness unlike anything she'd ever known rested on her tongue. Could this be what it felt like to kiss the feet of her Lord? She smiled in her dream state. This far surpassed any wild berries, even those sweetened with real sugar.

In the distance, Nettie heard the sound of a melodic choir. The inaudible words blended into a perfect harmony, echoing all around her. Where had the music come from? Why did she hear it in every direction? Maudie Mae played piano and sang beautifully, but these sounds were more perfect than any earthly refrain.

Nettie floated on through the clouds, relishing the smells, tastes, and sounds of this incredible experience. The brilliant dream wrapped her like a warm quilt in winter. How good of God to bless her with this glimpse of heaven. In the years to come as Abraham and Aaron grew, she'd never cease to remind them of this gift on the day of their birth.

A delicious thought swept over her. She didn't have to leave these clouds; she could dwell here forever. Riley and their sons could join her. They'd never have to experience pain or sorrow again. *Yes,* she thought. *I don't want this dream ever to end.*

≈

In the dark of the night, Mary crept from the room. She'd tended to the babies before leaving Riley alone again. The midwife had said nothing except to voice her thoughts on acquiring someone to nurse the twins.

"I don't want to think we'll need one," Riley said. "She's going to recover; I'm sure of it."

"Your faith is the type that creates miracles." The solitary candle silhouetted Mary's short body. The only other light in the room came from a silver moon casting its light through the window. "I took the liberty of sending Roy after Preacher Faulkner. I know God listens to all of us and doesn't show favoritism, but it can't hurt to have a man of God praying too."

"I'd welcome having the preacher here," Riley said. He stared at the babies, his sons. "Did Nettie tell you we named them?"

"Yes." Mary smiled and focused her attention on the infants. "Fine names, Mr. O'Connor."

"Riley."

"All right, Riley. She's right proud of those twins. I hated taking them from her to clean them up. . .and then later."

He released a pent-up sigh. "What caused the problem? Did I do something wrong?"

"No, not at all. Don't even think you're at fault. Things like this sometimes happen."

"She told me about drinking red raspberry and ginger tea, and she didn't have a hint of morning sickness or trouble during the carrying time," Riley said. "Other than craving sleep, she was just fine."

Mary stepped over and touched Nettie's forehead. "I gave her a mixture of yarrow and other herbs to drink, but the heavy bleeding hasn't stopped."

Riley gathered up Nettie's limp hand and kissed it. "You've done a powerful job, Miss Mary, and I thank you."

A faint knock at the door alerted him to the presence of a caller—Preacher Faulkner. Riley felt his hopes heighten at the sight of the man who had become such a good friend. Still dressed in the overalls he'd worn earlier that day, the godly man more closely resembled a farmer.

He knelt by Riley's side on the floor, as if the position was commonplace to him. "I'd have been here sooner if I'd known. How's she doing?"

Riley turned his head and offered his Nettie a faint smile. "She's quiet. Sleeping. Most likely telling the angels about her twin boys."

Preacher Faulkner peered up into Mary's face, but Riley pretended he didn't see the grave look of concern passing between them. "Nettie's a fine woman," the preacher said.

"She's strong too." Riley wondered if the added words were to convince himself or Preacher Faulkner. "Just look at those healthy babies."

Silence passed between them before the preacher placed a hand on Riley's shoulder. "I know you've been talking to God, but I'd like for us to pray together."

Riley bowed his head. For a moment he considered Preacher Faulkner might have the right words for God. Instantly he shoved the notion aside. Prayin' didn't mean fancy words. It was simply telling God what He already knew.

"Lord, we're asking You to heal Nettie," the preacher prayed. "She's had a powerful hard night birthing these babies, and she's almost too tired to fight. Riley here is scared, and their children need a mother. . . . I guess that's it, Lord. We've told You how much we care about Nettie and how we so much want her with us for a long time. It's mercy we're asking and strength for her to stay with us. In Your Son's holy and cherished name, amen."

"Amen," Riley whispered and opened his eyes. "Preacher, I've never told you, but I do like the way you talk to the Lord, real natural like He's having coffee with us or something."

"And how do you pray, Riley?"

He shrugged. "The same, I guess. You reassure me when I hear you talking to the Lord in the same way."

One of the twins whimpered, and Mary scooped him up into her arms and softly coaxed him to hush. Her tender voice soothed Riley as well.

"We named them already," he said.

Preacher Faulkner stood and examined the one in Mary's arms and the other who instantly grasped the man's finger. "And what are their names?"

"Abraham Riley and Aaron James," he said.

The preacher chuckled. "They look just alike. How are you going to tell them apart?"

"Nettie knew the difference and told me," Mary said. "I tied a bit of ribbon around Abraham's wrist."

Preacher Faulkner spent equal time with the twins. "James is my given name. No one's called me that for years, not since my dear mother departed this world." The moment the words left his tongue, the preacher gasped. "I'm sorry, Riley. Don't know what I was thinking."

"It's nothing. Nothing at all." *Stay with me, Nettie. Don't give in to this.*

ঽৡ

Nettie continued to bask in the heavenly dream. She loved the free sensation of being suspended among the clouds. Suddenly she heard another sound. The voice sounded like

Riley. He was praying for her. He didn't want to say good-bye. He begged God to return her to him.

This must have been the feeling all along, a dream of what she thought heaven might be. If only folks could feel the same perfect love weaving in and around their body and spirit.

She heard Riley again. He wept, and the sobs nearly broke her heart. One of the twins cried out. She'd miss their growing-up years. *Please, Jesus, I want to be with You, but can I go back to Riley and the babies for a little while longer?*

Her answer came in a soft breeze. It cradled her for a moment, like a newborn. How tempting for her to dwell in this embrace until she saw Jesus' outstretched arms. Nettie felt His words communicate His guidance and understanding. She would fight, for her time on earth was not yet finished.

Nettie felt strength returning to her body. Her mind resounded with one word: Jesus. On she fought. Her eyelids struggled to open. She tried and failed. She dared not give up.

At last a slit of light gave her the courage to go on. "Riley," she said and questioned whether she'd said his name or that her love had broken the barriers of time.

"Nettie!" He sobbed.

"Don't cry. I'm not leaving you."

His hand stroked her cheek as a tear trickled down. "You made it."

She did her best to smile, not knowing if the gesture reached her lips. "I couldn't leave without seeing Montana. . .and I couldn't leave you."

"I love you, Nettie."

"And I love you."

epilogue

"Is this it, Riley? Is this truly our land?" Nettie got up from the wagon seat. The twins slept peacefully in the back, surrounded by belongings that would mark their new home. She saw acres and acres of rolling green. The sky never looked bluer. The trees appeared taller, standing as sentinels to the portals of heaven on earth.

"This is our home." Riley had waited so long for her to see, even feel, the beauty of the ranch. "Our paradise."

"Oh, please, stop the wagon." She hopped down from the step even before he pulled the horses to a halt. "Riley, this is all you've ever said and more." With flushed cheeks, she whirled around. "Why, this even smells like a bit of heaven."

Riley laughed. "How would you know what heaven smells like?"

She flashed him a quick smile. "Someday I'll tell you."

"When are you going to tell me?" Sitting on the wagon seat, he watched his precious wife come alive with the surroundings. The sight made him want to burst.

She gazed up into a cloudless sky. "I'll tell you when you take me to the spot where we'll build God's church."

"I can hardly wait," he said. "Nettie." Her gray gaze captured his. "I love you."

A Letter To Our Readers

Dear Reader:

In order that we might better contribute to your reading enjoyment, we would appreciate your taking a few minutes to respond to the following questions. We welcome your comments and read each form and letter we receive. When completed, please return to the following:

Fiction Editor
Heartsong Presents
PO Box 719
Uhrichsville, Ohio 44683

1. Did you enjoy reading *Temporary Husband* by DiAnn Mills?
   ❏ Very much! I would like to see more books by this author!
   ❏ Moderately. I would have enjoyed it more if

   _____

   _____

   _____

2. Are you a member of **Heartsong Presents**? ❏ Yes ❏ No
   If no, where did you purchase this book? _____

   _____

3. How would you rate, on a scale from 1 (poor) to 5 (superior), the cover design? _____

4. On a scale from 1 (poor) to 10 (superior), please rate the following elements.

   ____ Heroine   ____ Plot
   ____ Hero   ____ Inspirational theme
   ____ Setting   ____ Secondary characters

5. These characters were special because?_____
_____
_____

6. How has this book inspired your life?_____
_____
_____

7. What settings would you like to see covered in future
   Heartsong Presents books? _____
   _____
   _____

8. What are some inspirational themes you would like to see
   treated in future books? _____
   _____
   _____

9. Would you be interested in reading other **Heartsong
   Presents** titles? ❏ Yes ❏ No

10. Please check your age range:
   ❏ Under 18   ❏ 18-24
   ❏ 25-34   ❏ 35-45
   ❏ 46-55   ❏ Over 55

Name _____

Occupation _____

Address _____

City_____ State_____ Zip_____

To Catch
A Thief

4 stories in 1

*I*n a time when women find career options limited, four Chicago women get the chance of a lifetime— busting a ring of train robbers for the Pinkerton Detective Agency. Working undercover in Windmere Falls, Colorado, they begin to unearth clues overlooked by their male counterparts. Nobody's expecting much from these female operatives—but breaking the case may take only some womanly intuition and a little faith. Will they ride the rails to success. . .and love?

Contemporary, paperback, 368 pages, 5 ³/₁₆"x 8 "

Heart♥ong

Any 12
Heartsong
Presents titles
for only
$30.00*

HISTORICAL ROMANCE IS CHEAPER BY THE DOZEN!

Buy any assortment of twelve *Heartsong Presents* titles and save 25% off of the already discounted price of $3.25 each!

*plus $2.00 shipping and handling per order and sales tax where applicable.

HEARTSONG PRESENTS TITLES AVAILABLE NOW:

(If ordering from this page, please remember to include it with the order form.)

Presents

Great Inspirational Romance at a Great Price!

Heartsong Presents books are inspirational romances in contemporary and historical settings, designed to give you an enjoyable, spirit-lifting reading experience. You can choose wonderfully written titles from some of today's best authors like Peggy Darty, Sally Laity, Tracie Peterson, Colleen L. Reece, Debra White Smith, and many others.

When ordering quantities less than twelve, above titles are $3.25 each.
Not all titles may be available at time of order.